ROSE'S WAR

Rose's War

ALISON DAVISON

SERENDIPITY

First published in 2004 by
Serendipity
Suite 530
37 Store Street
Bloomsbury
London

British Library Cataloguing-in-Publication data
A catalogue record for this book is available from the British Library

ISBN 1-84394-090-6

Printed and bound by Alden Group, Oxford

Dedicated to Roy and Charrise

Chapter 1

1941

Rose was in a good mood; her sister Joyce was home on leave from the Wrens and they were getting ready to go out for the evening. It had been a long time since the pair of them had been out together. Joyce had joined the Wrens just after the war had started. Rose would have liked to have joined up but she had been born with a leg deformity. One leg was longer than the other. It would have been a problem for some people but Rose hadn't known it any other way; it was part of being her.

When she had been young they had tried to operate on her leg to straighten it and it had been partly successful, but she still had a limp. Rose however was the happy-go-lucky type of person, never complaining, saying that there were worse off people than herself.

Joyce had become so used to wearing a uniform that she felt awkward in a frock.

'Rose, do you reckon this dress looks all right?'

'Yes, you look lovely.'

Rose had been ready for ages; she was wearing her favourite blue frock.

'Come on or else it will be midnight before we get out,' said Rose.

The girls walked over to the bus stop near their house and waited for the bus.

'I hope it's soon, I'm freezing,' moaned Rose.

'It should be here any minute now,' said Joyce.

They got the bus and got off near to the hall; the girls crossed the road and walked the short distance to the dance hall. They went in. It was packed with servicemen and they had trouble getting a table.

'Look, there's one over there,' Joyce shouted above the noise. They walked over to the table, took off their coats and sat down. Joyce said to Rose, 'You stay here while I go and get our drinks.'

Rose sat tapping her feet to the rhythm of the music. It was playing her favourite song, the 'Lambeth Walk', and she thought the band were really good. Rose noticed a group of servicemen laughing and joking, really enjoying themselves. The dance floor was packed with couples dancing and the place was full of smoke from cigarettes that lingered in the air.

Rose was looking around when she noticed a soldier looking at her from across the hall. She met his gaze for a second or two and he smiled at her; she looked away shyly.

'Here we go; god, it's murder trying to get to the bar,' moaned Joyce.

'Thanks, I think I've been eyed up by one of the soldiers over there.'

'What one?' asked Joyce, looking around the hall.

'The one by the window, standing with four others. Don't keep looking, he'll know we're talking about him,' Rose hissed.

'It's too late, it looks like he's coming over,' replied Joyce.

Before they could say anything else this tall, slim soldier with jet black hair came over to their table.

'Hello, would you like to dance?' he asked Rose.

'No, thank you,' she replied.

'Well, if not a dance can I buy you ladies a drink?'

'Thank you, that would be nice,' said Rose.

He asked what they would like and went to get the drinks from the bar.

'He seems nice,' said Rose, 'good looking too.'

Joyce wasn't so sure; he seemed too cocky to her.

The soldier came back with the drinks and introduced himself as Stanley. He signalled to his mate to come over. 'This is William, do you mind if he joins us?'

'No, that's all right by us,' said Joyce.

'Nice to meet you,' said Rose. 'This is Joyce and I'm Rose, we are sisters.'

'Please,' said Joyce, signalling for them to sit down.

'So you're both in the army, where have you been fighting?' Rose asked.

'We have both come back from abroad, we have got a week's leave,' replied Stanley.

'Well, it must have been hot, you've both got sun tans,' said Joyce. 'You both look like you've come back from a holiday.'

'I wish we had,' replied Stanley.

'It must be hard being away from home,' said Joyce. 'I know how it feels. I'm in the Wrens, and I'm stationed in this country.'

'Does anyone want another drink?' asked William. He took the orders and went to go up to the bar.

'I'll come with you,' said Stanley.

Up at the bar William said, 'So what one are you after?'

'The one in the blue dress, Rose, isn't it?' replied Stanley.

The evening went well and everyone enjoyed themselves dancing and talking. Before long it was time to go home. The boys offered to walk the girls back.

Rose had thoroughly enjoyed herself. It wasn't often that she got the chance to talk to a lot of adults. She was a nanny and spent most of the day around young children. Rose hadn't been out much since Joyce had joined up; she sometimes went out with her best friend Mavis but she preferred going out with Joyce. They would go everywhere together. When they had been children everyone referred to them as the Brown sisters.

Helping Rose into her coat Stanley asked, 'So where do you live?'

'Not far, we live in Chingford, do you know it?'

They set off with Joyce and William ahead of them at a discreet distance. They talked along the way about what they did, who they lived with. Rose was normally the shy one out of the two sisters but with Stanley she found she could talk to him with ease.

They reached the row of terraced houses where the sisters lived and once outside the gate to their house William asked Joyce if she would like to see him again.

'I'm sorry but I won't be able to. I'm only home for a week and then I'm going back up north. I would really like to spend some time with my family, but thank you for asking. I have really enjoyed your company tonight.'

'Well, goodnight, Joyce, maybe some other time.'

'Well, 'night all,' said William before he walked off into the night.

Joyce felt awful saying no but she had seen so many people get hurt when the servicemen were killed in action and she didn't want to get involved with anyone in the forces; it was safer that way, she had told herself.

Joyce said goodnight and told Rose that she would see her indoors. She let herself into the dark house then she shut the door.

Rose stood outside the house, not sure whether to go in or not. She had turned to let herself in when Stanley said, 'Rose, will you see me again?'

'Yes, that would be lovely.' She tried not to appear too pleased; she didn't want him to think that she was desperate.

'Will tomorrow night be convenient?' he asked.

'Yes, I'm not doing anything,' Rose replied.

'I'll come by and pick you up at seven then.'

He kissed Rose and then said goodnight.

Rose let herself into the house and closed the door. She felt as if she was floating on air; she was so happy he had asked her out she couldn't stop smiling.

'Well, I don't need to ask if you're seeing Stanley again, your face says it all,' said Joyce.

Joyce wasn't happy about Rose seeing Stanley. She thought he seemed a bit too smooth, and thought he would end up hurting Rose. She had seen his type often enough, but when she had tried to tell her when they had gone to the ladies that night Rose had brushed it off by saying that he was just confident. Rose was already smitten, much to Joyce's horror.

Joyce knew there wasn't much point in saying anything more to Rose. She knew how determined she could be, so Joyce left it at that.

'We're going out tomorrow night. Are you going to see William again?' Rose asked.

'No, I'm not,' replied Joyce.

'Why, I thought you two were getting on really well, didn't he ask you?' Rose asked.

'He asked but I said no.'

'Why didn't you want to see him then?' Rose asked.

'There is no point getting involved with someone at the moment. I'm going back next week; it wouldn't be fair on him or me.'

Rose couldn't understand her sister sometimes: she would never let anyone get too close; it was as if she was afraid to get involved with anyone.

'Well, I don't know about you but I'm ready for bed,' yawned Joyce.

'I'm coming just after I've had a drink,' replied Rose.

Joyce reached the top landing and was just about to go

to bed when her mother called out from her bedroom, 'Is that you, Joyce?'

'Yes, Mum,' she answered back.

'Is Rose with you?' Ethel asked.

'Yes, she's downstairs having a drink.'

Ethel got out of bed and went into the girls' room. 'Did you both have a good time?'

'Yes, Rose had a better time though. She has met a soldier, who she's seeing tomorrow night,' Joyce replied while she tried not to yawn.

Kissing Joyce goodnight Ethel went downstairs to see Rose. Her curiosity had got the better of her and she wanted to hear all of that night's events.

Sitting in the front room cradling a hot cup of tea and looking as if she was miles away Ethel said to her, 'Well, I can see you had a good night by the smile on your face, so who is he then?'

Rose smiled at her mother and said, 'Mum, he's lovely, he's a real gentleman. He pulled out the chair for me and held the door open; he was so easy to talk to, Mum.'

'He sounds nice, are you going to see him again?' Ethel asked.

'Yes, tomorrow night, he's meant to be picking me up at seven o'clock.'

Ethel went and made herself a cup of tea and sat down with Rose and heard all about the night.

'Didn't Joyce meet anyone tonight?' Ethel asked.

'Yes, she did, but when he asked to see her again she said no.'

'That's a shame, she always keeps them at arm's length, she's frightened to get involved with anyone,' sighed Ethel. 'I often wonder if she will ever settle down.'

'Give her time, Mum, maybe she'll meet someone when this damn war is over,' said Rose.

They drank their tea and then went to bed.

'You all right, Ethel?' Percy asked when she returned to bed.

'Yes, I have been talking to our Rose; she's going out tomorrow with a soldier,' Ethel replied.

'Let's hope he's a good one, I know what they can be like,' Percy replied.

'Well, I'm sure our Rose will behave herself, she's a good girl,' Ethel said.

'That's not what I meant,' Percy said.

Ethel knew what Percy was getting at. He had been a soldier in the First World War and he knew what they were like. Luckily for her she had married a good one. Percy had been Ethel's childhood sweetheart and they loved each other deeply. Things hadn't been easy for Percy: his mother had tried to get him to marry for money not love but he wouldn't hear of it. He flatly refused to go along with his dominating mother's wishes, which had enraged her. His mother had tried to bribe him by telling him that unless he married Violet Price, a wealthy landowner's daughter, the house she had built for him as a wedding present would be withdrawn. Percy had chosen Ethel and had moved into Primrose Terrace, a rented house, much to his mother's disgust. Percy was disinherited from his mother's will. Sometimes Ethel felt guilty. If it hadn't been for her Percy could have had an easier, more comfortable, life. Ethel hated her mother-in-law.

Ethel just wished Joyce could feel that way about someone herself.

Sunday afternoon Rose went round to see her best friend Mavis to tell her all about the previous night's events. She had promised to tell her all about it, as Mavis should have gone with them but her mother had been ill and she couldn't.

'Well, did you meet anyone then?' Mavis asked.

'Yes, he's a soldier on a one week pass,' Rose said excitedly.

'What does he look like then?' Mavis was excited for her friend and a little disappointed that she had missed out on meeting someone herself. The pair of them had gone up to Mavis's room to talk in private away from her pesky brother.

'Well, he has got black hair, blue eyes, he's very tall and slim,' Rose told her. 'He's ever so handsome, I can't believe my luck,' she said excitedly.

'Did he kiss you?' Mavis asked.

'Yes, he did, right outside my doorstep.'

'Mavis, can you open the door for me; I've made you and Rose a drink,' said Mavis's mother Gladys.

'Thanks, Mrs Smith,' as Rose took the steaming cup of tea.

'You girls are cheerful, what you up to?'

'Rose has met someone, Mum,' replied Mavis.

'Good for you, Rose, about time you met someone nice.'

'How are you today, Mrs Smith?' Rose asked.

'I feel a lot better today, thank you, Rose, my chest infection's almost gone.'

Mavis and Rose finished their tea and Rose said, 'I'd better go. Stanley is seeing me tonight.'

Mavis saw Rose to the front door and let her out. 'Thanks for coming round, Rose, I'll see you tomorrow if you're not busy.'

'All right, after work about six,' Rose said as she started to walk back to hers.

That evening Rose was so nervous she was like a cat on a hot tin roof. She was rushing around trying to decide what to wear for her date with Stanley.

'Joyce, help me find a frock.'

Joyce went upstairs with her and helped her decide what to wear.

'What about this one?' Joyce said, holding up a green frock. 'You look nice in this.'

'No, can I borrow your flowery one?' Rose asked.

'All right but don't get it mucked up, it's my favourite,' replied Joyce.

They didn't own many clothes and they often borrowed each other's things. Things had been tight before the war but trying to get new clothes these days was often a nightmare, thought Rose; even if you had the clothing coupons or money it was hard trying to find anything half decent to wear.

The ships that were bringing over food and other merchandise weren't getting through; they were being torpedoed by enemy submarines, so they had a constant shortage of certain foods.

'Bloody sods.' Percy was sitting in his favourite armchair listening to the news on the wireless.

'Percy, stop swearing,' Ethel scolded him. She hated her husband swearing in front of Fred, their young son.

'Sorry, love, another ship's gone down, all those poor souls lost at sea.'

'I don't know why you listen to that, it's constant bad news. I wish they'd have happy news for once; we could do with cheering up.'

'Dad, do you think we'll win this war? asked Freddie.

'I don't really know, son, it don't seem like it at the moment.'

'Dad, you was in the First War; what was it like?' Freddie asked.

'It was terrible, son, I wouldn't wish it on anyone.'

That wasn't the answer Freddie wanted to hear; he was eleven years old, the age when you thought it was brilliant being a soldier. However Percy knew differently; he was lucky to be alive after being gassed in the trenches. He could still visualise it in his mind's eye, the death of his friends who they had to leave where they fell. He had come back a hero and been given medals, but he had thought that he was lucky to come back at all.

After half an hour Rose came downstairs and almost wore the carpet out with her constant backwards and forwards in the front room.

'Will you please sit down, Rose,' her mother said.

'Sorry, Mum, I'm really nervous; what if he doesn't turn up tonight?' she anxiously said.

'Well, if he doesn't then he isn't the right one for you,' replied Ethel.

'There's plenty more fish in the sea,' said Joyce.

'He's late, he isn't coming,' Rose said.

'Just give it a few more minutes,' said Ethel.

Just after seven o'clock there was a knock at the door. Rose got up quickly to answer it.

'Rose, slowly, you don't want him to think you're desperate,' her mother scolded as she sat knitting. Freddie, Rose's brother, beat her to the door and opened it.

'Hello, is Rose there?' the man asked.

'Rose, there is someone for you!' shouted Freddie, just as Rose came into the hallway.

'Are you ready?' Stanley asked.

'I'll just get my coat.' Rose went into the front room, kissed her Mum and Dad goodbye and went into the hall for her coat and bag.

'I thought we'd go down to your local pub; is that all right with you?' he asked.

Rose nodded and said, 'That will be fine.'

Chapter 2

The Fox and Hounds was quiet, not many people were in there. Rose was glad; she hated it when it got crowded. They went and sat in the snug and Stanley went and got them a drink. It was nice in there with the roaring fire and cosy chairs to sit in.

Stanley came back with the drinks and sat opposite Rose. 'Here you go, sorry I was late; I got held up.'

'Well, at least you're here now,' replied Rose, sipping her drink.

'So what have you done today, anything nice?' he asked her.

'No, nothing special, me and Joyce helped out at home. I've got this week off from my job.'

'Oh, what do you do?' he asked, supping his pint of best.

'I'm a nanny for a local family, I've been there for years,' Rose replied. She was holding her drink and running her finger around the rim of the glass.

'Do you like it, working with kids all day?' he asked as he supped his pint.

'Yes, they are lovely children, well behaved. You got any brothers or sisters, Stanley?'

'Just one brother, I haven't seen since this war broke out. He's in the army as well.'

'Do you miss him, then?' Rose asked.

'No, not really, we never really got on,' replied Stanley.

'I really miss my family, especially Joyce, we are really close. I haven't seen my brother George for a year. He should have come home six months ago but his leave was cancelled at the last minute. We write every week though. I just pray he stays safe,' Rose said.

'What's he in?'

'The army, the Royal Signals,' Rose replied.

'They have had a bad time of it recently, I've heard on the grapevine,' said Stanley.

'Yes, I know they have lost a lot of men. George can't say too much but he did mention that to us. We don't know where he is stationed.'

'We are the same. We have to keep it a secret in case Jerry gets to hear,' Stanley said.

All of a sudden the air raid alarm started to go. Stanley pulled Rose out of her seat and shouted, 'Quick, we've got to get out of here!' They ran out of the pub to see what was going on. Bang! Something had been hit close by from the sounds of it.

'It looks like Primrose Terrace has taken a direct hit,' someone said.

It happened within minutes; there hadn't been much warning before the bomb had hit its target.

'No,' shouted Rose as she ran towards her home. Stanley ran after her just as she reached the end of the terrace. Her leg was killing her but she didn't stop running, thinking only of her family's safety. She was frantic for news of their whereabouts.

'Rose, stop her,' shouted Stanley, and catching hold of her arm he pulled back as another explosion ripped through the houses.

'Let me go, my Mum and Dad are in there!' she screamed, trying to get out of his vice-like grip.

'It's not safe, we will find them soon but you can't go right now,' he shouted at her.

Stanley held Rose back; she sobbed in his arms.

After a few minutes the emergency services arrived and

pushed everyone back from the flames. It was busier than Piccadilly Circus with firemen and ambulance men trying to get to people. Rose hoped her parents had gone down to the Anderson shelter as they normally did when the sirens went off; she knew her mother hated the shelter but she would go down for her father's sake; though he sometimes had to force her into it. Rose just hoped that they had made it out in time. The bomb had hit before a proper warning had been given.

When they had dug the air raid shelter out everyone was moaning what a tedious job it had been but the thing had most certainly saved lives. It was made out of corrugated iron, with mud thrown on the roof. A lot of people grew vegetables or flowers to brighten them up but the Brown family left theirs bare. Ethel always felt claustrophobic in the shelter. She had a really bad problem with small spaces and considering it was only 6 feet by 12 feet with at least four people at any one time in it she hated going into it. Hearing the air raid siren go off was terrifying at the best of times but it took all of Ethel's willpower to go down into it.

Percy had said to Ethel one day after they had got the all clear to come out, 'You are lucky, gel, we have got our own shelter. A lot of poor buggers have to go down and sit it out with strangers in the underground stations, all squeezed together for the night. How would you like that?'

Ethel had agreed that sounded far worse than what they had to put up with and tried not to moan so much when they had to go down there.

When it had rained a lot the Anderson shelter would flood with water that had drained down from the reservoir; they would wake up in the morning and their things would be floating in a massive puddle. Ethel was terrified that one day the damn thing would cave in on them.

Rose could tell that next door had been badly damaged

and one near the end of the terrace. She didn't think her house had been hit but she couldn't be certain as the smoke was too thick and had obscured the view. The house next door had been badly hit by incendiary bombs and was now a pile of rubble. Rose just hoped that Mrs Clarke had got out in time. Everyone who lived in the terrace was moved across the road while an assessment was made of how badly damaged the houses were.

Rose stood with Stanley amongst the crowd asking if anyone had seen her parents but no one had. She was beginning to lose hope when one of her neighbours said,

'Rose, look, there they are.'

She ran to them and after hugging and kissing them she learnt that luckily they had heard the siren and dashed out of the house with barely seconds to spare. They had only just got into the shelter before the bomb had exploded next door.

'Cor bloody hell, that was a bit too close for comfort,' said Percy. He was helping Ethel who was in shock and had a vacant expression on her face that Rose had never seen before.

'Mum, are you okay?' Rose asked, hugging her.

'She's in shock. We'd best find her a blanket and a cup of sweet tea,' said Joyce.

'I'll go and see if anyone's got one we can borrow,' said Percy. He came back with a pile of blankets that someone had given him. 'Here, put this around your mother and see if anyone else needs one.'

Joyce took the blankets from her father and put one round her mother.

'Here you go, Mum, you best sit down.' Leading Ethel over to the grass verge she sat her mother down on the side of the kerb and sat with her and Freddie.

Rose took the rest of the blankets and handed them out to some of the elderly residents.

'Thank you, Rose, love,' said Mrs Jenkins as she took the blanket.

'Here you are, love, you get this inside of you,' said one of the women who lived near to where Ethel and Joyce and Freddie were sitting. She had come out of her house with a tray of tea and was handing it around. 'Bloody awful thing to happen this time of the night, in this weather too,' the woman grumbled. The wind whipped around everyone, making their teeth chatter.

Joyce took a mug of tea and gave it to Ethel.

'Here, Mum, drink this,' she said as she put the cup to her lips. Ethel started to drink the tea with a little help from Joyce.

'How do you feel now, Mum?' Joyce asked.

'A bit better, ta,' Ethel replied. 'Where's your dad and Rose?'

'They are around here somewhere; don't worry, they are safe,' said Joyce as she rearranged the blanket around Ethel's shoulders.

'Mum, are you all right?' Freddie asked. It had frightened him, seeing his mother like this.

'She's going to be all right, Freddie, she's just in shock from the explosion,' said Joyce.

Rose came back after handing out the rest of the blankets.

'Here, I saved you this,' said Joyce as she handed a mug of tea to Rose.

'Thanks, I'm bloody freezing,' she said. 'I wish this wind would die down.'

'Where's Stanley gone?' asked Joyce.

'He thought he'd go over and see if they needed a hand with anything,' replied Rose as she sipped the warm tea, holding her hands around the mug to try and warm them up a bit. 'God, you had me worried when I couldn't find you; I thought you had all been in the house when that bloody bomb hit our terrace.'

'Lucky we was quick or else we would have been. We got out into the garden as it hit next door's. Just as well we were all downstairs at the time in the back room; we only had to run out of the door,' explained Joyce.

'Dad made us walk all the way round the back,' grumbled Freddie.

'That's because he wasn't sure the house was safe to walk through after the blast,' said Joyce.

'Ethel, are you all right, love?' Percy asked when he returned.

'Yes, dear, I feel better now.'

'I'm going to see if they need any more help,' said Percy. 'Look after your mother for me.'

After Percy had gone all the rest of the family sat down and waited to hear what was happening to them that night.

'I don't reckon we'll be allowed home tonight,' said Joyce. 'They will probably send us to the local hall for the night at least.'

'Did anyone see if old Mrs Clarke made it out?' Ethel quietly asked but they barely heard her.

'We don't know, we haven't seen her,' replied Rose.

The volunteers searched through the rubble trying to see if anyone was alive. Almost everyone had been accounted for except Mrs Clarke who hadn't been seen since the explosion. Everyone held their breath with anticipation. Everyone was saying how lucky they all were; it happened so quickly they were amazed there hadn't been more people found dead.

'Someone must have been watching over us,' said Mrs Jenkins, crossing herself in a crucifix sign and kissing her rosary beads that hung around her neck.

They all knew what old Mrs Clarke was like: she was a stubborn old fool sometimes and had made it clear she wasn't going to sit in the shelter, saying no one was going to force her out of her home, not even the Germans.

'They have found someone,' shouted old Mr Jenkins. 'Looks like it could be old Mrs Clarke.'

'That bloody old fool, I told her time and again to go to the shelter, did she listen?' cried Ethel.

'It's not your fault, Mum, you tried your best,' said Joyce, hugging her mother while she sobbed. They all watched as they brought a body out from amongst the rubble and laid it gently on a stretcher, covered it over and carried it away into an ambulance. Percy came over with a grim look on his face and said, 'They have found her; she was trying to get out of the kitchen door by the looks of it.'

'Oh, the poor woman,' cried Ethel.

'She had her cupboard too close to the kitchen door, she always had a habit of doing that; no wonder she couldn't get out in time,' said Rose.

The rescue services and the volunteers worked through the night trying to make the site safe. They were busy putting out fires from when incendiary bombs had exploded. They hadn't done too much damage, luckily, except for Mrs Clarke's which had taken the full blast. It was obvious they weren't allowed home that night so they were taken to the local hall and slept in blankets on the floor or on fold-up beds. The houses had to be checked for structural damage before they could go back in to them.

'Bloody uncomfortable laying down here,' grumbled Mr Grey.

'What would you rather have, this or a wooden overcoat?' someone shouted out.

Every one was quiet after that comment; they knew they were lucky to be alive. So far they all had homes to return to, but many hadn't.

There had been a lot of discussions about what had happened that night. Some thought the bomb was meant to hit the ammunitions factory two miles down the road, others reckoned it was aimed at the reservoir. That would have had devastating consequences had that been hit; the whole area would have been flooded and it would have depleted almost all of London's drinking water causing major problems on top of the problems they already had.

In the morning they went back to see what was happening at Primrose Terrace. In the clear light of day it didn't look too bad. All of the fires had been put out and there was the smell of burnt wood in the air but Mrs Clarke's had been badly hit; it was a pile of rubble. Thankfully, no one else's had been hit, but one life was one too many and it was a bit too close for comfort when you actually knew the person that had died. It made the war seem more real, more personal, thought Rose.

'You okay, Rose?' Joyce had seen Rose shudder when they had seen what next door's was like. Joyce had seen what the war could do: being in the Wrens she had seen the aftermath of lives literally ripped apart. It had hardened her a little but Rose was blissfully unaware. Until now she hadn't experienced any part of the war, and now she didn't like what she saw.

'Come on, let's get in and sort our place out,' said Ethel. She didn't want to linger there too long. It just upset her seeing where her neighbour had died the night before.

The Browns picked their way through the hallway to see what sort of mess awaited them. Percy had been working almost all night and looked exhausted. Stanley had too; he came and said to Rose that he was going home to sleep, Rose said goodbye to him and then went to help her family with the clearing up.

'Has Stanley gone?' asked Ethel.

'Yes, just a few minutes ago,' replied Rose.

'That was nice of him to lend a hand like that last night,' Percy said.

'Are you seeing him again, Rose?' Ethel asked as she got the broom from the closet.

'Yes, he said he will be round tonight to take me out.'

'That's good, he seems like a nice enough bloke,' said Ethel.

Ethel and Joyce were sweeping up all of the glass and putting it in bags. Percy boarded up the windows and Rose tried to make breakfast which didn't involve using the gas and electricity. They had been switched off again to prevent another explosion. All Rose could do was butter some bread and boil some water on the little paraffin stove which they used for times like these.

'Mum, breakfast's ready!' shouted Rose.

They sat where they could and ate and drank while discussing what had to be done that day. Freddie was horrified to find out that he was being sent to school that day and had moaned about it to his mother; however Ethel was not in the mood for his whingeing and told him life wasn't fair so he had better shut up before he got a clout around the ear from her. Freddie stomped off to school with the sulks; he hated it. As Rose saw Freddie out of the front door she noticed someone had placed a bunch of flowers outside Mrs Clarke's house; they were white lilies. Going back into the house, Rose said to Ethel and Joyce, 'Someone's put flowers down on next door's garden, I wonder who that was?'

'Well, whoever did that, it was nice of them,' replied Ethel.

'Mum, do you think we ought to put some there?' asked Rose.

'Don't see why not,' Ethel replied. 'We have got some nice roses in the garden. I'll cut some later and put them outside the house.'

Later that day Ethel went out into the garden and looked for the best roses she could find. She chose some white ones and cut a dozen or so; she put them into the basket she was carrying and took them into the house to show the girls.

'Mum, they're lovely,' said Rose.

'Come on, we'll put them there now,' said Ethel.

Ethel, Joyce and Rose went outside and placed the flowers next to the others and then went back inside the house. By nightfall next door's front lawn had been covered in flowers that others had laid in memory of old Mrs Clarke; it seemed fitting considering the circumstances.

'Life still has to go on despite the war,' sighed Percy as he went off to work. The girls helped their mother to finish tidying the house and by the afternoon it looked habitable again. Except for the boarded up windows and the roof tiles missing it didn't look too bad. At least they still had a home to tidy up, thought Ethel.

'Not exactly a nice welcome home is it?' her mother said to Joyce.

'At least I know you're all safe; that's all I care about,' Joyce said.

That night Stanley came round to take Rose out again. They decided to go for a walk in the park. They were both wrapped up in coats and gloves as it was late September and the nights were turning cold. There was a distinct nip in the air as winter was creeping up on them. There would be no leaves on the trees soon, thought Rose; she hated wintertime – it was depressing to her. They were walking silently along by the duckpond holding hands when Stanley said, 'Rose, next week I've got to go back, my leave will be up; will you write to me while I'm gone?'

'Yes, of course I will,' Rose replied as she held his hand; she had hoped he'd ask that.

The couple spent every spare moment that they had together, going to the pictures, for walks and having a drink in the pub before Stanley's leave was up.

On the final night Rose couldn't help feeling sad. She had only known Stanley a week but she felt as if she had known him forever.

'What's wrong, you're abnormally quiet?' he teased.

'Nothing,' she replied.

He didn't press her but asked, 'You will still write, won't you?'

'Yes, of course I will, I'm just sad that you have to go away, that's all.'

'I wish I could stay, but I haven't any choice.' He turned to her and said, 'I will miss my English rose.'

Stanley kissed Rose with so much passion it took her breath away. He held her close; it may have been cold but the intensity of their love had kept them warm.

They said goodbye to each other and Rose watched him go until he was out of sight. With a heavy heart she went inside and closed the door. She wondered if she would ever see him again.

Rose wrote to Stanley regularly without fail, telling him all the local news. She tried to keep the letters light-hearted but she knew by the reports on the wireless that they were having a bad time fighting. Germany seemed to be winning and she prayed every night that Stanley stayed safe. His letters were few and far between. Her mother had warned her that they would be like that but it was hard for her waiting to hear from him. Every time the postman came she rushed out to meet him only to be told, 'Sorry, Rose, nothing for you today.'

'Do you think he's forgotten about me?' Rose asked her mother over breakfast one morning.

'No, I'm sure he hasn't,' said Ethel. 'It's the post, it's never regular during war. I remember waiting to hear from your father just like you are now. I would get upset and then out of the blue I'd get two or three at once, so stop worrying, Rose.'

Rose felt better hearing that and decided to take each day at a time. She tried not to think about Stanley but every so often she would do something that reminded her of him, or conversations they had had or things they had done.

One day she was putting some ironing away and was thinking about him. This is stupid, she thought to herself, I hardly know him.

His letters were a lifeline of their love and she couldn't get enough of them, Rose's life was on hold until she received the next letter from Stanley and she got to know the postman really well: so much for letting go, she thought to herself.

Ethel had said to Rose one day, 'It's harder for the women at home; all they can do is wait and worry about what's going on. The men accept that they have got a job to do.' Patting Rose on the shoulder she said, 'I know what you are going through.'

Two weeks later Rose received three letters all at once, scribbled in Stanley's handwriting. She eagerly tore open the letters and started to read.

He wrote that he was missing her and thinking about her and couldn't wait to see her. Her letters kept him going in this damn place which he described as hell.

Rose was pleased that he still had feelings for her, though she hadn't seen him for months. She continued writing to him.

Suddenly all of Stanley's letters stopped. Rose was terrified that he had been killed or captured. She waited to hear from him but unknown to her Stanley had been mildly injured and was in a military hospital. He had been shot in the arm he wrote with and couldn't write to let her know. It was weeks before he could pick up a pen again and write. Rose hadn't heard from him for more than a month when out of the blue she received a letter from Stanley's friend

William explaining why he hadn't written to her, and she didn't know whether to feel relieved or worried. At least she knew that he was alive which put her mind at ease. She had sat at home and thought of terrible scenarios about what had happened. Rose wondered if this was what her mother had gone through with her father.

Rose wrote back to Stanley after hearing about him being shot and said that he didn't get out of writing to her that easily. He had laughed when he had read that.

One Saturday morning a year after Rose had started to write to Stanley there was a knock at the door. Percy went and answered it and said, 'Rose, you had better come out here; someone wants to talk to you.'

Rose went to the door expecting it to be her friend Mavis. Letting out a scream, Rose said, 'When did you get back?'

'Yesterday,' Stanley replied.

'It's so good to see you again, Stanley.'

The couple kissed and hugged and then she remembered her manners and invited him in. 'How long have you got this time?' she asked.

'Just another week and then I'm going back. Come on, get your coat, let's go for a walk.'

'Where are we going, Stanley?'

'I'll tell you when we get there.'

They got the bus and he rang the bell at the stop near the park.

'Come on, we get off here.'

'We're not sitting in the park, are we? It's too cold, you must be mad,' cried Rose.

It was the middle of September and rapidly moving towards autumn. There was a chill in the air and the leaves had begun to drop off the trees and crunch underfoot as they walked.

'Stop moaning and come with me. Do you remember the last time we were here, Rose?'

'Yes, a year ago on your last night.'

Stanley walked her over to the bandstand and said, 'I have got something to ask you.'

'What is it?' Rose asked, wondering what he was going to say.

Stanley got down on one knee in front of her and asked, 'Rose, will you marry me?'

Rose stood frozen to the spot: did she hear right?

'Well?' he asked.

'Yes.' She was too shocked to say anything else. 'Have you asked my father?'

Producing a small box, he opened it, took out an engagement ring and put it on her finger. 'Don't worry, it's been sorted out. I have already asked your dad for his permission.'

Rose hadn't needed her father's permission to get married as she was twenty-six years old but she was glad that he had; it showed respect.

'When did you do that?'

'When you were in the kitchen helping your mother make the lunch today.'

'I wondered why it was a bit quiet when we came back in. I thought you and Dad had had words.'

'Well, we did,' he said, laughing.

Hitting him, she said, 'You know what I meant.'

'Well, do you want to go home now and tell them the good news?'

'What do you think?'

Grinning, she held onto his arm and said, 'Come on, it's freezing out here.'

Chapter 3

Rose and Stanley got the bus back to her house to tell everyone the good news.

'You're back early,' her mother said when they entered the front room.

'There is something we need to tell you.'

'Oh,' said Ethel, looking up from her knitting.

'Stanley and I are getting married.'

Ethel was shocked. She hadn't seen this one coming at all.

'Congratulations,' said Percy.

'You knew about this, didn't you, Percy?'

Smiling, he said, 'It's about time I knew something you didn't, woman. Ethel, go and get the glasses, we are having a toast.'

'So when are you getting married?' Ethel asked, coming back into the room with the glasses in her hand.

'Next week,' Stanley said.

'Next week, we need longer than that!' Ethel cried.

'Sorry, Mrs Brown, but I'm only home for a week and then God knows when I will be home next.'

'Mum, I'm sure we can do it if we have a small wedding,' Rose said.

'I have got a special licence so we can get married quickly,' Stanley said.

'Why all the rush?' asked Ethel suspiciously. Ethel thought, she can't be pregnant, she hasn't seen him for over a year; at least it wasn't that. 'You barely know each other; why not wait until this war is over?'

'Mum, we don't know when that will be; we love each other, we don't want to wait.'

Ethel looked at Rose's pleading face and all her reserve melted away. After a moment's thought Ethel said, 'I'm not happy about you rushing into this marriage but I can't stop you.'

Rose was over twenty-one years old and could get married without their permission but she didn't want Rose doing that so she had no alternative but to go along with Rose's wishes. Running off getting married on the quiet would have looked as if she had something to hide so she said, 'Looks like we have a wedding to arrange.'

Rose hugged her. 'Thank you, Mum.'

'Welcome to the family, son,' Percy said, congratulating Stanley. Percy had no problem with it, thought Ethel, so why should I?

After Stanley had gone Rose dashed round to tell Mavis her good news. She knocked on her front door and waited impatiently for someone to answer.

'Hello, Rose, do you want to see Mavis?' asked Gladys. 'You best come in.' Shutting the door behind Rose she shouted out to her daughter, 'Rose is here to see you.'

Mavis came running down the stairs. 'You all right? It's a bit late making house calls,' Mavis said, fiddling with the rollers in her hair.

'Sorry if I got you out of bed but I had to tell you my news. Guess what, I'm getting married.'

'Rose, that is wonderful. Mum, did you hear that? Rose is getting married!' Mavis shouted out.

Gladys came into the hallway. 'Did I hear right? Congratulations, Rose, when's the big day?'

'Next Friday,' cried Rose.

'That soon, what did your mum say about that,' asked

Gladys. She was surprised at the quickness of the wedding and did wonder if she was in the family way.

'Mum was a bit shocked but Stanley is only home for a week and we wanted to do it before he goes back,' replied Rose. 'Well, I better be going, see you soon, Mavis, bye, Mrs Jones.'

Shutting the door after Rose had gone Gladys said to Mavis, 'Rose isn't pregnant, is she?'

'Ooh Mum, why do people always ask that? No, she's not, they just love each other, that's all,' replied Mavis angrily. She thought that it was really romantic and wished it was herself getting married like Rose.

The next day was Saturday so Ethel and Rose went into town to see if they could find the material for her wedding dress. They knew it wouldn't be easy but after walking from one shop to another they had to admit defeat. Rose was beginning to panic.

'Mum, what am I going to do if I can't find any decent material?' Rose said, almost in tears.

Ethel thought of an idea and said, 'What about my wedding dress? I know it's old fashioned but what if we alter it for you, do you think that would work, Rose?'

'Mum, you can't chop up your wedding dress, what about the sentimental value?'

'I only kept it in case my daughters might wear it one day. If you want it you can have it. I really don't mind, in fact I would be pleased.'

Rose had always liked her mother's wedding dress and when she was a child at special times her mother would let her dress up in it. 'Mum, that would be lovely,' said Rose.

'Right, then let's look for a pattern and see if we can alter the design of the dress,' said Ethel.

'I could do with a cuppa,' Ethel said after they had spent

nearly all morning scouring the shops. It wasn't easy as the shops had next to nothing in them thanks to the war.

They found a pattern Rose liked in one of the big shops in town and they decided to stop for tea.

'I'm parched,' said Ethel to Rose. 'All this walking around is thirsty business,' as they sat in the tea shop and drank a large pot of tea. 'Come on, let's finish off and get the bus home.'

Exhausted from all of the walking they flopped into chairs. After half an hour they were refreshed enough to go upstairs and get Ethel's wedding dress. Ethel took it out of the wardrobe and unwrapped it from all the tissue paper. It was over twenty years old but it was still in perfect condition.

'Rose, try it on,' said Ethel.

Rose took it from her mother and put it on. It was a little long for her and Rose was a smaller size than her mother, but it could easily be altered. Rose loved the material and was pleased Ethel had suggested it.

Ethel said, 'Come downstairs and I will see what I can do.'

After looking at the pattern they had bought that day it was decided that Ethel would alter the neckline and the sleeves and also the low waistband that was so fashionable in the nineteen twenties, so she got to work pinning and taking it in while Rose stood in the front room on a chair with the dress on. When she had finished. Rose changed out of it and Ethel started to cut and sew while Rose supplied cups of tea. She was terrible at sewing and didn't trust herself enough to start now.

Ethel was handy with a sewing machine; with four children she needed to be. She had made most of their clothes when they had been small. Ethel worked on the dress all that afternoon, only stopping to make their tea, and she returned to it straight afterwards while Rose washed up the dishes.

At last it was finished and Rose tried it on for the final fitting. 'Oh Mum, it's lovely, thank you.' Rose was admiring it in her mum's long mirror in her bedroom.

'I'm glad I kept it but I'm even happier to see you wear it,' Ethel said. 'I'm just glad I didn't need to make your dress from scratch as I'm not sure it could have been finished in such a short time, so maybe it was a blessing we couldn't find the material. You had better go and take it off now, Rose; I need to finish it.'

Ethel took it back downstairs and finished the final details on it before handing it over to Rose. Rose took it upstairs and hung it on the back of her bedroom door.

'Well, that's the dress done. We'd better sort out the food for the reception. I thought you might like to have it here considering it's going to be a small wedding.'

'Thank you, Mum, that would be lovely. I'll tell Stanley tomorrow when he comes round.'

The next day Ethel popped into her neighbours' to tell them the good news and to ask for some help with getting the food for the wedding. Most of the food she could get. The family owned a farm so they were luckier than most and never went without fresh eggs or milk.

Ethel spoke to her friend Rene to see if she could bake the cake. She was delighted and said it could be her wedding present to Rose and Stanley. She could supply some of the ingredients but Ethel would have to get her the eggs and butter, as these were in short supply.

'Right, that's the dress and cake sorted out. Rose, what sort of things do you want to eat at the reception?'

'Nothing much, just some sandwiches, meat and whatever we can get.'

'I'll get your father to go to Granddad's farm and see what he can do,' replied Ethel.

The family farm was small with sheep, pigs, chickens, geese, eight horses and the odd goat and rabbits, which they bred for eating. They were lucky and ate better than most people considering the war.

Once all the neighbours heard about Rose getting married they volunteered their services by giving her ration stamps towards the buffet. Rose was overwhelmed by people's generosity. That night Stanley came to see her and she told him about the day she had had. Stanley had been to the church of St Mary's and had spoken to the vicar about the marriage. It was all arranged for that Friday, which gave them four days to get everything done.

After Stanley had left, Rose asked if they would be ready in time for the wedding with half a week to go. Rose wasn't convinced it would be done in time. Had she asked too much of her mother by doing this so quickly? She felt guilty. Her mother had done too much already and she loved her mother very much.

They were sitting down having a rest when Rose said, 'It's a shame Joyce and George will miss my wedding. It won't be the same without them.'

'Why don't you send Joyce a telegram? said Ethel.

'I never thought of that, thanks, Mum,' Rose said excitedly.

Rose decided no time like the present and rushed off to catch the bus into town. She wrote a short message to Joyce which read, 'Come home this Friday. Getting married. Rose.'

'Well, did you send the telegram to our Joyce?' asked Ethel when Rose returned.

'Yes, I just hope she gets it,' said Rose.

Joyce received the telegram from Rose and almost fainted in shock when she read it. What was she doing getting married to that idiot? she thought. She sent a telegram back saying she would be there. Joyce had been given permission and had been given a twenty-four hour pass.

Rose received the telegram and showed it to her mother. 'Look, she can come,' she said excitedly.

'See, I told you Joyce would make it. It's a pity George can't though,' said Ethel.

Rose decided to write and tell George all about the wedding so he didn't feel so left out. He had been fighting somewhere abroad. She didn't exactly know where, just that it was in the desert, maybe Egypt or Africa: they never knew.

Chapter 4

Rose had received another telegram from Joyce saying she should be home Thursday night, around eight o'clock. Rose hovered around the window facing the main road, waiting for Joyce's bus to come in. She had a good view from the bay window and waited. She anxiously watched every single bus that passed by. 'She did say eight, didn't she?' Rose asked for the tenth time.

'Yes, she'll be here,' said Ethel.

A little after eight a bus pulled in and Joyce got off it.

'She's here,' said Rose as she rushed to the front door to welcome her. Hugging her, Rose said, 'I'm so glad you could come; it wouldn't have been the same without you there.'

'Well, I couldn't miss my big sister's wedding, now could I?' Joyce said.

'Have you eaten, love?' asked Ethel to Joyce.

'No, I'm famished.'

'Sit yourself down and I'll rustle something up.'

'Hello gel, we're glad you could come to see your sister married off,' said Percy, giving Joyce a fatherly hug.

The atmosphere was buzzing with excitement as everyone in the family chatted about the up and coming nuptials. Rose was the first one in the family to get married out of her three siblings.

'Here you are,' said Ethel as she came into the room with a plate of chicken sandwiches for Joyce. 'Go and make a pot of tea, Rose, while I have a chat with Joyce.'

Rose took herself off to the kitchen to make the brew.

'Well, how was the journey?' asked Ethel.

'Not too bad, it's a pity I'm so far away from home. I miss everyone,' replied Joyce as she ate her sandwiches. 'Mum, these are lovely, did the chicken come from the farm?'

'Yes, where else? We have got chicken for tomorrow's buffet, your Granddad sent a whole load up today. Everyone has been so helpful, helping with the food.'

'Here we are,' said Rose as she brought a tray of tea things through.

'Well, this is hardly fitting the occasion. Ethel, go and get some glasses and we'll open a bottle,' said Percy. He uncorked a bottle and started to pour. Once all of the adults had a drink in their hands a toast was made. 'Here's to our Rose, we hope you find true happiness,' said Percy. 'Cheers.'

'Good luck, Rose,' said Freddie as he gave her a hug. Rose kissed him on the cheek and ruffled his hair. 'Thank you, Freddie,' was all she could say before she was overcome with emotion and started to cry.

That night Rose and Joyce sat in their bedroom and talked, while they sat on Rose's bed.

'Are you sure you want to get married?' Joyce asked.

'Yes, of course I'm sure,' replied Rose.

'You haven't known Stanley very long.'

'Don't you like him?' asked Rose; she so wanted her sister to get on with her soon-to-be husband.

'Yes, of course I do,' Joyce lied. She didn't want to upset her sister by telling her the truth, but in actual fact Joyce thought Stanley was a bit shifty and she didn't trust him. What was the hurry? She couldn't pinpoint exactly what it was about him other than when you spoke to him he seemed vague and not very talkative about his family which to Joyce seemed funny because their family were very open and loving about each other. Joyce was always talking about her family.

When Joyce had pointed this out to her mother some

time ago her mother had said not everyone liked to talk about their family and maybe Stanley didn't get on with his. After that conversation with her mother, Joyce kept her opinions to herself. Joyce wasn't trying to be nasty but she loved her sister and didn't want to see her get hurt.

'Is Stanley's family coming to the wedding?' asked Joyce.

'No, he told me his mum and dad were killed during a blitz at the start of the war and his brother is serving in South Africa in the Army.'

'That's a shame, it would have been nice to meet them,' replied Joyce. She was thinking to herself that it seemed convenient. Rose was so happy Joyce had to go along with the charade.

They talked all evening about hopes and dreams and what they wanted from the future. All Rose wanted was to become a mother. Her job since she had left school was as nanny to the Austin family who lived a mile away. She loved the children whom she had looked after since their births.

'You two had better get some sleep,' Ethel said, 'or else you will have bags under your eyes in the morning and you don't want that, do you?'

The girls said goodnight to their mum and dad and got ready for bed.

It was a shame that Rose decided not to have a hen night: even if they had gone for a drink it would have marked the occasion, after all you only got married once, but Joyce knew Rose hated to be the centre of attention.

'Joyce, do you think I'm doing the right thing marrying Stanley?' Rose asked as they lay in their beds.

Joyce hesitated before she answered, then said, 'Do you love him?'

'Yes,' replied Rose.

'Well, you can't be doing the wrong thing, then.'

'Thanks,' said Rose before falling asleep.

'Rose, wake up, it's seven o'clock,' said Ethel.

Rose opened her eyes and said, 'What time is it?'

'It's time you were up, the tin bath is full of boiling hot water and if you don't get up soon it will go cold.'

Rose got up and stretched before going downstairs for her bath; she noticed Joyce had already got up. The house was a hive of activity. Her mother was scolding Freddie for getting his best shoes dirty, Joyce was ironing some clothes and Dad was polishing his shoes.

After Rose had her bath she sat down and Joyce did her hair for her, brushing it and putting in some hair clips to keep it in place. She didn't need a lot done to it as she always kept it short in a bob; she couldn't be bothered like Joyce with perms and rollers.

Rose went back upstairs to put on her wedding dress. She stood and admired her mother's handiwork before taking it off the wooden hanger and putting it on.

'Is it all right to come in?' Joyce asked, standing outside the closed door.

'Yes.'

Joyce walked in with her freshly ironed clothes in her hand and stood and stared at Rose standing in her wedding dress in the middle of the small bedroom that they had shared all their lives.

'Well, what do you think?' she asked.

'Oh it's lovely. Mum did a really wonderful job on making your wedding dress,' sighed Joyce.

'Well, hopefully one day Mum will be making yours too,' said Rose.

'Are you ready, you two?' Ethel called from downstairs.

Joyce grabbed her handbag and went downstairs. 'Mum, you did a wonderful job on Rose's dress.'

'Well, where is she then?' asked Percy. He had come out into the hallway just as Rose was walking down the stairs. 'You look lovely, petal,' he said.

'Mum, the car is here to take us to the church,' said Freddie, rushing in from outside the front garden.

'Well, we'd better be going,' said Ethel as she gave Rose a kiss. 'See you there, love.'

After everyone had left to go to the church Percy said, 'Rose, are you sure you want to go through with this? It's not too late to pull out if you want,' he said.

'No, I want to marry Stanley, Dad.'

'All right, I just had to ask.'

Any doubts Rose had were gone and she couldn't wait to marry Stanley.

'Well, the car's here, shall we go?'

They came out of the house and some of the neighbours had come to wish Rose good luck. As she got into the car her friend Mavis shouted, 'See you when you get back, good luck, Rose!' Mavis had been invited to the reception after the wedding and was going to help put out the food for the buffet with her mother's help.

At the church of St Mary's Stanley was waiting nervously in the church with his best man.

'Look, here come Rose's mum and sister,' said William. 'Rose will be here,' he said, trying to reassure Stanley.

Ethel, Joyce and Freddie took their places at the front of the church and waited for Rose to arrive. There weren't many going to the wedding. Almost all the young men were away at war so it was mainly family and friends and a few neighbours who had been invited. Ethel just hoped Vi, her sister-in-law, had made an effort: she worked on the family farm and was usually covered in feathers from the chickens she plucked. Ethel prayed she'd had a bath as she didn't want her stinking the church out with the smell of manure. Vi was certainly a character, thought Ethel to herself.

Ethel quickly looked around the church to see who had turned up. Luckily Vi had dressed for the occasion and Ethel was relieved to see no feathers in sight.

Percy's mother was sitting in the second row looking her usual snobby self. She gave Ethel a nod and looked away; there was no love lost there. Ethel felt sorry for Percy's father; she wore the trousers in that family. Charlie always looked anxious to her; it was a shame as he was a lovely bloke and it was no wonder he took refuge in a bottle of Jack Daniels whenever he could.

Jack, George and his wife Rene and Tom and his wife Ginny were there in the third pew.

As Stanley stood with his best man people had whispered how strange it was that no relatives of Stanley's had been invited. Surely he must have had aunts, uncles or cousins: it seemed strange to them, it didn't add up.

Someone shouted from the front of the church, 'They're here!'

The car pulled up and Percy helped Rose out, Rose held her father's arm and stood at the door and waited for the music to start.

'Well, here we go, pet.'

Stanley turned round to see Rose walking down the aisle. He thought she looked lovely as she walked down the aisle to him.

Rose reached Stanley and Percy stood back and sat down with Ethel.

The vicar coughed and cleared his throat.

'We are gathered here today to witness the marriage of Stanley and Rose.' He went through the ceremony and then asked, 'If there is anyone against this marriage speak now or forever hold your peace.'

Stanley looked around nervously: was anyone going to speak?

All was quiet and the vicar carried on with the service. At last they were married and the happy couple came out of the church for some photographs before heading back to Ethel and Percy's for the reception.

'Oh, look at all the food; I haven't seen so much since before the war,' Rose's aunt Ginny said.

Between Rose's family and neighbours they had managed to put on quite a spread. They had sandwiches, sausage rolls and cakes. It was handy having grandparents that owned a farm so they were lucky to get things that others couldn't like eggs and meat. Ethel would barter with her friends and neighbours for things they couldn't easily get.

Rene, her mother's friend, had done a wonderful job making the wedding cake even if she had to use a cardboard cover because she couldn't get hold of icing sugar to decorate it with.

At the reception Percy stood up and banged his glass to get everyone's attention.

'Ladies and Gentlemen, I would like to thank you all for coming and putting on such a lovely spread; I haven't eaten that well since before the war.' Everyone clapped in agreement. 'I would like to say how proud I am, we are, of our Rose and we hope Stanley takes care of our little girl.'

Rose had to hold back the tears when her father had said that.

They cut the wedding cake and after everyone had eaten, it was time for Stanley and Rose to leave. They were just staying in a hotel for the night because Stanley had to be back at the barracks the next morning or else he would have been classed as a deserter and arrested.

Rose had wished that they had longer to celebrate but they had just one night, so William drove them to the hotel.

'See you tomorrow, Stanley, try not to be late.'

Rose and Stanley got the key to the room and went in, Rose felt really nervous; she hadn't done this before. Kissing her after he shut the door on the outside world Stanley eagerly started to undress Rose. Soon she was down to just her underwear. She felt shy and it must have showed because

Stanley took her hand and sat her on the bed where she quickly got under the covers.

He undressed and got in with her. Whatever he's doing feels good, thought Rose.

They had made love and afterwards Stanley held her in his arms.

'That was your first time, wasn't it?' he asked her.

Rose looked at him before answering, 'Yes, it was.'

'Well, we better put in some practice then,' he cheekily replied.

Laughing, they dived back under the covers.

Chapter 5

The following morning Stanley woke Rose. 'Come on, sleepy head, you have got to get up.'

'Do I have to, it's so early,' replied Rose.

'Yes, afraid so,' Stanley said as he got dressed into his uniform. 'I have got to be back at the barracks by nine o'clock but before then I have got to get you home.'

Stretching, Rose got up and went to get ready.

Stanley caught her arm and pulled her towards him, kissing her passionately. Laughing, Rose said, 'I thought you were in a rush.'

'I don't care now, I've seen you in your underwear, the army can wait.'

They made love again and then it really was time to go. Rose hurriedly got dressed and they left the hotel and went back to her parents.

Stanley and Rose went into the house and Stanley picked up his kitbag from the hallway, kissed her goodbye and left.

Waving at him as he went, Rose couldn't help feeling sad. They had hardly had a honeymoon, had they? She waited until she couldn't see him any more and went inside the house. Her mother was in the kitchen baking so Rose sat on the steps leading down to the kitchen. She would sit there when she was a young girl and watch her mother working in the kitchen; that way she kept out of her mother's way but could still watch. The kitchen was tiny and you could only fit two people in there at once.

It was also the bathroom; when you needed a bath you had to get the tin bath in from the lean-to and fill it with boiling water. They didn't have an inside bathroom but they had an outside lav, which was freezing in the winter and boiling in the summer. Rose hated the spiders that frequented there. Once one had fallen into her lap and she'd never moved so quickly in all her life. The family loved teasing her about her phobia especially her younger brother Freddie.

'You all right, Rose, you don't seem to be very happy?'

'I'm fine, Mum. I just wish we could have had a proper honeymoon. He's promised we will have one when this war's over but it won't be the same.'

'I know, it was the same with your Dad and me. We only got away after he was demobbed and by then I was expecting you. People must have thought we had a shotgun wedding; still it gave them something to talk about, I suppose.'

Rose laughed 'So there were three on your honeymoon then?'

A week after Stanley had gone Rose got a letter from him. She took it upstairs to her bedroom and read it while she sat on the bed. He had written the day he had left; she knew because of the date at the top of the letter.

My dearest Rose

Thank you for becoming my wife, I'm sorry we could not have a honeymoon, but like I said we will go away as soon as this war is over, whenever that will be. They have sent me abroad again but I can't say where I am but it is hot and sandy. The place is full of sand flies which buzz around you all day long, getting in your eyes and down your throat, but I try to take my mind off them by thinking about you, my perfect English Rose. I hope everyone is well, say hello to Ma and Pa, Freddie and Joyce from me.

I can't wait to see you and make up for lost time. Love you with all my heart.

Love Stanley

Rose blushed when she read the last line; he was referring to their night in the hotel. She had felt so shy she couldn't get undressed in front of him without blushing with embarrassment. Her mum had tried to talk to her about what was expected of her but she felt awkward and just said that if she didn't want to get pregnant Stanley should use something: that was it. Rose knew less than she did before. Rose never brought it up with Stanley that night as she felt too embarrassed to ask him.

In another letter Stanley asked Rose to look for a flat for them for when he came home on leave, so they would have some privacy. He liked Rose's family but he was married to just Rose not the whole family. Rose went downstairs after reading the letter and said to Ethel, 'Stanley wants me to find a flat.'

Ethel was surprised; she had thought while Stanley was away Rose would be staying at home with them. She felt upset that she was going to leave but tried not to show it by saying, 'Oh, we thought you'd stay here until Stanley came home for good.'

'I need to leave home sometime, Mum.'

'Yes, I know that,' said Ethel while she washed up in the kitchen. 'Won't it be lonely all on your own?'

'No, I don't think so. I'll be at work and I can pop in and see you most days.'

'Well, it looks like you've already made your mind up. When will you start looking?' asked Ethel.

'I have got a day off on Monday, so I might as well start then.'

Rose went to see Mavis, her best friend, to see if she knew anyone who was letting anywhere.

'Well, I don't know anyone at the moment but if I do find out of anywhere I'll let you know.'

The following Monday Rose took Ethel with her to look at some places for rent. After looking at four places that were too small, too pricey or too far away, she had to admit defeat. 'God, you couldn't swing a cat in that last place and the amount of money they wanted was criminal; what am I going to do, Mum?'

'All you can do is keep looking; something is bound to come up, just give it time.'

That night Mavis came to see Rose. 'Did you find anything today?' she asked.

'No, I didn't,' said Rose dejectedly.

'Well, I found out today that there might be a flat for rent above the newsagent's down the High Street. Do you know Mr Smith who owns the newsagent's, Rose?'

'No, not really,' replied Rose, 'do you?'

'Yes, he's a friend of my dad's; why don't we go tomorrow and see if it's true,' said Mavis. 'I'll meet you tomorrow after work, you finish at four o'clock, don't you?'

'Yes, I'll knock for you after four o'clock and then we can go together,' said Rose.

Rose told Ethel about the possibility of a flat above the newsagent's that she was going to enquire about the next day with Mavis. She sounded excited when she told her mum.

The following day Rose couldn't wait to leave work as she wanted to find out about the flat. She really hoped it was available as it would be perfect for her. She tried not to get her hopes up too much in case Mavis had got it wrong.

'Well, are you ready?' asked Rose, who had just knocked for Mavis.

They caught the bus to the High Street and walked over to the newsagent's shop.

'Hello, Mavis, what can I do for you?' Mr Smith asked.

'Is it true you have a flat for rent?'

'Yes, why, you fed up with living at home, Mavis?' he asked.

'No, it's not for me, it's for my friend Rose here; she's looking for a place.'

Mr Smith looked Rose over and said, 'You married, young lady?'

'Yes, I am,' replied Rose.

'That's good, I don't want a load of men in and out all day and night,' he sniffed.

'Rose ain't like that; she's a respectable woman with a husband who's in the army,' Mavis said.

'All right, you can go and take a look.' He handed the keys to Mavis. 'It's number six. You need to go round the back way and up the stairs and along the corridor to the end.'

Mavis took Rose up to the flat. 'Here we are,' she said as she opened the front door. Rose walked into the hallway and looked around. It was a good size with a front room which had a brown armchair, a settee and a coffee table and it overlooked the High Street. The kitchen was tiny with a gas stove and a few cupboards and a table to work at; it was clean and tidy. Rose looked in the bedroom which was sparsely furnished with a bed and an old wardrobe. It was perfect. She liked the bathroom which was the first one she had seen in a house.

'This is perfect,' said Rose. 'It's big enough for me and Stanley; how much do you reckon he wants for it?'

'Well, let's go and ask,' said Mavis. They locked up and took the keys back down to Mr Smith.

'Well, what do you think?' he said after he had served a customer in the shop.

'It's just what I'm looking for; how much do you want for it?' asked Rose.

'Well, how does a pound a month sound?' he said.

'That would be fine, do you want a deposit or something?' asked Rose.

'Yes, I ask for one month's rent in advance and a small deposit in case anything gets damaged. Is that all right with you? Normally I like to have references before I let people rent my places but being as you're a friend of Mavis's I'll let you off.'

'So when can I move in?' asked Rose.

'Any time you like, it's vacant now,' he said.

'What about this Saturday?' asked Rose.

'Yes, okay, as long as you pay me.'

Rose opened her bag and took her purse out, counted the money out for the month's rent and deposit and handed it over to Mr Smith.

'Wait there and I will give you a receipt and a rent card.'

The girls waited in the shop. Rose couldn't stop smiling; she was so happy she wanted to rush home and tell her mother. After a few minutes Mr Smith came back with the paperwork and gave it to Rose.

'Thank you, Mr Smith,' said Rose as she stuffed the receipt and rent card into her bag.

'Mavis, make sure you say hello to your dad and mum for me.'

As they left to walk out of the door Mavis said, 'I will, cheerio.'

'Oh, thank you,' said Rose once they were outside the shop. She was so happy she gave Mavis a hug. 'You'll have to come round for dinner after I have moved in and celebrate with me.'

'You're on, I'll keep you to that,' said Mavis as they waited for their bus to come.

'Mum, Dad, guess what, I've got a place to live, thanks

to Mavis,' she blurted out after bursting through the front door. 'I can move in on Saturday.'

Ethel and Percy looked at each other before Ethel said, 'Where are you moving to?'

'That place I told you about yesterday, over the newsagent's in the High Street. Dad, do you think you could help me move my stuff in?'

'I don't see why not, I'm not working on Saturday.'

'Thanks,' she said, giving her dad a hug.

'So what's it like?' Ethel asked. She was worried; she hoped Rose hadn't been conned into renting a rat's nest.

'If you like, I'll show you it after tea,' Rose said eagerly.

They ate their tea and Rose helped her mother to wash the dishes, and then they all set off to take a look at the flat Rose was moving into.

'Well, what do you think?' asked Rose, after showing her parents and Freddie around.

'It's very nice; you have made a good choice,' said Ethel. She was relieved to find that it wasn't some seedy hovel her daughter was going to rent.

'Well, what do you think, Dad?' Rose asked.

Percy had kept quiet. 'Well it looks like our little girl is leaving home.' He was upset, he hated it when any of his children left home; how had they grown up so fast? he wondered.

That night after they got back home Rose started to pack some of her things ready for that weekend. The rest of the week couldn't go quickly enough for Rose, she was so eager to move into the flat. It wasn't because she hated living at home; she just felt that it was time to get a place of her own.

'Well, what do you think about our Rose moving out then?' asked Ethel to Percy as they got ready for bed.

'Well, to be truthful I'm not very happy about it. It's not like Stanley will be living there full time with her, but she's a grown woman now; it's not down to us any more,' he said sadly.

'Rose where do you want this?' It was Saturday and Percy was bringing in her few sticks of furniture.

'In the bedroom near the wardrobe,' Rose said while she and her mother cleaned the kitchen from top to bottom. It was clean and tidy but Ethel insisted on doing it, saying, 'You don't know who lived here before, some people have got filthy habits.'

It didn't take long to settle in. She was grateful to have the flat partly furnished as she didn't own a lot of furniture. They all finished what they were doing and flopped into chairs for a well earned rest.

'I'm famished,' said Rose.

'So am I,' piped up Freddie who had been a really big help in bringing up the furniture with his dad.

'I'll go and put the kettle on,' said Rose.

'While you're out there, get some plates, would you, Rose,' Ethel said.

Rose made everyone a cup of tea and took some plates through. She hadn't had time to get anything in, and wondered what her mum had in mind.

Going into her big bag Ethel produced a homemade cake; it was a real treat that they only had on special occasions. 'Well, who wants some cake?' she asked.

They all did; she didn't have to ask twice.

'Mum, this is delicious,' said Rose.

'Well, I thought this would be a special occasion for you living in your first home,' said Ethel.

'Mum, is there any more?' asked Freddie.

Ethel cut everyone another piece. After they had eaten Percy said, 'We'd better make a move.' They got ready to go home and kissed Rose goodbye they left.

Rose watched them go and when they had waved goodbye

to her she shut the door and went to wash up. The flat fell silent. Rose had never known it to be so quiet at home; there was always someone there. This would take some getting used to, she thought.

'Do you suppose Rose will be all right?' Ethel asked Percy.

'Yes, I'm sure she will be fine, but it's going to feel weird not having her around all the time,' said Percy.

'You've still got me, Dad,' said Freddie as they drove home; he was feeling a bit put out with all the talk about Rose leaving home.

'We are glad you're not old enough to leave home just yet,' said Ethel.

The following day was Sunday so Rose walked the mile to her parents' house. It had felt weird thinking that it wasn't her house any more.

'Hello, pet, get settled in last night all right?' her father asked as she came into the house.

'Yes, thanks, Dad, thank you for helping me; where's Mum?'

'She's out the back hanging some washing out.'

Rose went out to help her. 'Hello, Mum, do you need a hand?'

'Yes, please, love, how was the flat last night?' Ethel asked.

'It was okay, a bit quiet; luckily we never had a siren go off, I was dreading going down an unfamiliar shelter with a bunch of strangers. It will be all right once I get to know some of them.'

Rose stayed almost all day; it wasn't as if she had anything or anyone to rush home to.

Rose was just going up the stairs to the flat when a woman was walking down them. They met on the stairs.

'Hello, have you moved into number six?' she asked Rose.

'Yes, I have, I'm Rose.'

'I'm Vi, nice to meet you. Sorry I can't stop but I have got to get to work; maybe you would like to pop into mine for a cuppa some day soon. I live at number five.'

'Thanks, I'd like that,' replied Rose.

''Bye then,' and with that she shot down the stairs.

Rose let herself into her flat and put the kettle on. That night she wrote to Stanley to let him know the address of the flat. She told him all about it, saying she couldn't wait for him to see it; she placed the letter in an envelope and wrote Stanley's name and regiment and 'care of GPO' on it. She posted it the following day.

A few weeks after writing to Stanley she received a letter from him, saying how pleased he was that she'd found somewhere for them to live. He would be home on leave soon and he couldn't wait to see her and their flat. Rose was glad he had been pleased, and couldn't wait for him to come home; it had been six months since she had seen him.

One morning Rose was at the flat cleaning it when there was a knock at the door. She went to answer it, wondering who could be calling this early. She opened the door and standing there was Stanley. 'Glad to see me?' he asked.

'What do you think?' she said, melting into his arms. 'God, I've really missed you!'

'Well, you going to let me in or keep me on the doorstep?' he finally said.

Rose led him into the flat and shut the door. Dropping his kitbag on the floor he grabbed her and kissed her passionately against the wall.

'Well, where's the bedroom then?' he asked as he picked her up in his arms. Holding him around the neck, Rose giggled and pointed to the doorway at the end of the hall. Stanley carried her into the bedroom and laid her down on the bed. He quickly undressed Rose and himself and was just about to get down to some serious love making when Rose said, 'Quick, shut the curtains.' She was horrified in case anyone saw them in a compromising position.

He got up and pulled the curtains together. Smiling at her he then pounced on the bed. Kissing her all over he said, 'I've dreamt about doing this for months.'

Before he got down to the final act Rose asked, 'Have you got anything?'

Stanley looked at her with a confused look on his face. 'Got what?' he asked.

'You know.' She felt embarrassed; she didn't want to actually say about protection and she hoped he would.

'Oh no, I forgot, it will be all right,' he said, continuing where he had left off.

After they had made love he sat up in bed and had a smoke. Rose covered herself and snuggled up to him. 'I'm glad you're home,' she said happily.

Later that afternoon Rose got up and made them something to eat, then they sat on the settee in the front room.

'I've got to go out later,' he said.

'Why?' asked Rose. 'You have just got back, can't I go with you?'

'No, sorry, you can't.' He looked agitated. 'I promise I won't be long.'

Rose felt hurt; she hoped that his first night home they would have done something special together.

He left her at seven that night in a cloud of secrecy, refusing to say where he was going. Rose sat at home that night feeling miserable. Where was he, he'd been out for hours? Rose looked at her watch: it was past eleven o'clock. She sat waiting, all the while getting annoyed for being treated like this: what was so important, wasn't she important enough? she wondered.

At last she heard him at the door. Rose went to open it.

He was so drunk he couldn't find the keyhole; he staggered in through the front door.

'Stanley, where have you been?' she asked.

'None of your business,' he snarled back.

Rose shot back as though she'd been physically burned. This wasn't the man she had married, was it?

'Why won't you tell me; I was worried about you,' she whispered.

He lurched over to her and with his face close to hers said, 'Why don't you shut up?'

Rose wanted to move away from the stench coming from his mouth; it was making her feel like retching it was so bad. He stood above her and said, 'What's wrong, got nothing to say?'

'You're drunk,' she said, moving away from him.

'Oh, you don't want to be near me now, do you?' he said sarcastically.

'No, I don't,' Rose hit back.

Out of nowhere a fist hit her in the face, whack. She staggered backwards.

'Not so high and mighty now, are we?' he said as he kept hitting her.

She tried to protect herself by covering her face with her arms. 'Stanley, stop it,' Rose screamed. He seemed to come to his senses and stopped and fell backwards into an armchair; he'd passed out cold. Rose grabbed her coat and rushed to the door as quickly as she could. She limped away as tears fell down her cheeks and automatically headed towards her parents' house. She couldn't think straight. She took a wrong turn down a road; she was angry with Stanley and even angrier at herself for forgetting the way home. She had done this walk almost all of her life, she should know where she was going by now, she thought miserably.

She hated herself. She never thought something like this could happen to her. She'd often heard of other women getting hit by boyfriends or husbands and had thought that they had been weak to put up with it; she had thought at the time that if anything happened to her like that she'd hit them back, not just stand there taking it. She felt weak and pathetic as she wandered around the streets. It was freezing cold but she didn't care; she kept looking back over her shoulder to make sure Stanley hadn't followed her. The streets were deserted as closing time had been and gone at the pubs. She was glad; she didn't want to bump into anyone she knew.

Chapter 6

Rose opened the gate and let herself into the dark house. Her parents had probably gone to bed hours ago as it was after midnight by the time she had got there. She sat down in the dark front room and cried. She had kept the tears in while walking home, anger had kept them back, but now the anger had gone and the tears had come cascading down her face like a mini waterfall. She had her pride, she wasn't going to let Stanley see her cry.

'Rose, is that you?' her mother said, coming down the stairs.

'Yes, Mum,' she replied.

'What has happened, why are you here at this time of night?' Ethel switched on the light and gasped when she saw Rose's face.

'Rose, who did this to you?'

'Stanley did. Oh, Mum, he was so nasty to me, he hit me.'

'He hit you, why?' Ethel asked.

'We had a small row as he came back drunk; he hit me when I asked him where he had been.'

'Did he tell you where he'd been, Rose?'

'No, Mum, he said it was none of my damn business, that's what started the row in the first place. He only came home today, he's got so secretive all of a sudden.'

'He hit you for just asking that, I think you should tell your dad about this, Rose,' her mother fumed.

'No, I can't, we need to sort this out ourselves,' cried Rose.

'Well, I think you're being silly, what if he does it again?' sighed Ethel.

'It was because he was drunk, that's all.'

'Let's hope he doesn't make a habit of getting drunk very often then,' said Ethel, a bit sharper than she intended to say.

'Mum, I promise you if he ever hits me again then I will tell Dad.'

'You promise, Rose.'

'Yes, I promise, Mum, I will.'

Ethel went and got something to clean her up with. She came back with some antiseptic and some cotton wool. 'This might hurt a bit,' she said, dabbing at Rose's face.

'Ouch, you're not kidding!' cried Rose.

'Shush, you will wake your father.'

Ethel finished cleaning her up and boiled the kettle for a cup of tea for them both.

'Ethel, are you coming back to bed?' Percy shouted down to her.

Ethel shouted, 'I'm making myself a cuppa, I won't be long.'

'I'll come down then; I could do with one myself.'

'No, stay up there, I will bring it up in a minute,' she called out. 'Rose, you had better stay here tonight. When I go up, you go into your old room and stay there until your father goes to work and Freddie has gone to school; I'll let you know when the coast is clear.'

Ethel made the tea and took Percy's up to him.

'You were a while, who was you talking to?' he asked.

'Just the dog, that's all, he needed to be let out.'

'You all right, Ethel?'

'Yes, I just couldn't sleep that's all,' she lied as she sipped her tea.

Rose sat on her old bed and sipped the boiling tea; it hurt like hell and she had to stop herself from crying out in pain. So this is how it felt to be a punch bag, she thought to herself miserably.

The following morning Ethel got up and made Percy and Freddie their breakfasts, seeing Freddie off with a kiss. Ethel waited for a few minutes before calling Rose down. Sometimes Freddie would come back because he had forgotten something or other; he was a real scatterbrain.

'Rose, you can come down now, the coast is clear!' shouted Ethel.

Rose went downstairs and sat in the front room.

'You look tired; did you get any sleep last night?' Ethel asked.

'No, not really, I kept thinking about the row we had last night.'

'Rose, I'm worried: what if he had hit you so hard he'd killed you or something.' Ethel was worried for her daughter's safety. This was a side of Stanley they had never seen.

'He is being sent back in a few days' time. I have got to go home, I don't want Dad to worry; he has got enough to worry about without me burdening him with my problems.'

'He's your dad, it's our job to worry about our children even when they are all grown up, so no, you are not burdening us; like we said when you got married, we are always here for you.'

'Thank you, Mum.'

'Rose, this is the first and the last time I cover for you. A marriage is based on trust and I have never lied to your father up until last night. I won't do it again, do you understand?'

Rose nodded. After breakfast she washed up for her mother, then put her coat on ready to go home.

'I better go, Mum.'

'Take care, and remember what I said about us being here for you.'

Rose kissed her mother goodbye and left.

Ethel wasn't keen on her going home; God knew why she wanted to go back to Stanley after what he had done. It worried her no end but she knew how headstrong Rose could be: she was just like her father, too stubborn for her own good.

Ethel got back to doing the housework thinking about Rose; she really did worry her sometimes, but all she could do was be there for when she needed someone's shoulder to cry on.

As Rose walked home she got a lot of inquisitive stares from people when they saw her face covered with cuts and bruises. She tried to pull her collar up to cover her face. Every step was a step closer to home and she dreaded what she would find when she got there. She hoped Stanley would be out; she didn't want to see him.

She got to the front door to the flat, opened it and went inside. She was lucky – this time no one saw her come in; she would have died of shame if they had.

'Stanley!' she called out. No reply. Good, he must have gone out. She took her coat off and hung it up on a peg by the front door and went and looked in the mirror. God, he had done a really good job on her face; no wonder people had been staring. Her lip was cut and she had a swollen eye and bruises all over her face that were black and blue. She looked as if she might have been sent to the front line to fight in the war by mistake. She made herself a drink and was sitting down when Stanley came back. He looked at her face and stared in disbelief; he didn't remember hitting her that hard.

'Rose, I'm really sorry I hurt you, it was the drink,' he said lamely. 'Where did you go?' he asked.

'Home,' said Rose.

'I thought this was your home?'

'Not if that is what happens every time you have a drink it isn't,' she replied angrily.

'I promise it won't ever happen again. Look, I bought

you these.' He produced a bunch of flowers from behind his back and gave them to her. 'I'm really sorry, Rose.'

Rose took the flowers and said, 'Don't expect a bunch of flowers can excuse you for what you did, Stanley Noble, you go to hit me again and I will leave you as sure as a heartbeat.'

'We are still friends, aren't we?' he said, pulling a stupid face at her.

She hesitated before walking over to him. He took her into his arms and kissed her.

'Ouch, that hurt,' Rose said as she pulled away from his mouth.

'I'm sorry, will a cuddle do instead?' He held her tight and said, 'Do you forgive me?'

'I suppose so,' Rose replied.

The last few days Stanley had at home he treated her like a queen. He did the shopping, cleaned the flat and wouldn't allow her to move a finger. Rose knew it was because he felt guilty but she was enjoying seeing him squirm. She had to admit he was always gentle in the bedroom.

Three days later Rose helped him pack his kitbag and kissed him goodbye. She watched him go up the road until he was out of sight, then she walked away from the window.

That afternoon Rose had a visit from her mother. As Ethel entered the flat she said, 'Has he gone?'

'Yes, Mum, he went this morning.'

'Blooming good job he has gone, otherwise he would have got a piece of my mind,' replied Ethel as she sat down. 'So what was he like when you came home?'

'He was sorry, he said he wouldn't do it again,' replied Rose as she fidgeted nervously.

'He better not,' said Ethel tartly.

Ethel could see Rose was getting upset, so she said, 'Let's try and give him the benefit of the doubt and try to forget had has happened, what do you say?'

Chapter 7

Three weeks after Stanley had gone Rose went shopping with her mum. They had just came out of the butcher's shop where they had waited ages in the huge queue for their meat ration for the week when all of a sudden Rose said, 'Mum, can I sit down, I don't feel so good.'

Ethel was just about to reply when Rose suddenly keeled over and passed out in the street. Ethel bent over her daughter and tried to bring her round, and someone said, 'I'll go and get the doctor from Forest Road.'

'Quick, is the doctor here, a woman has collapsed in the High Street,' panted the man to the receptionist.

'Wait here, I will go and tell him.' The receptionist got up and knocked on the doctor's door. 'Excuse me, Doctor Roberts, there seems to be an emergency.'

The doctor grabbed his medical bag and rushed down the road with the young man to where Rose was. Rose had just come to when he got there.

'It's Rose, isn't it?' he asked.

'Yes,' she replied weakly.

'Rose, what happened, can you remember?' asked Doctor Roberts.

'No.'

Looking at Ethel he said, 'What did she do before she passed out?'

'She just said she didn't feel well and then she just passed out, Doctor.'

'Rose, can you walk?' he asked.

'Yes, I think so,' she replied.

'Let's get you over to my surgery; I can take a better look at you there.'

They managed to get Rose up, and Ethel thanked the young man for getting the doctor, as they left to go to the surgery.

Ethel waited in the waiting room while Rose was being examined.

The doctor took her pulse and her blood pressure and asked plenty of questions and to Rose's embarrassment gave her an examination before telling her, 'Congratulations, Rose, you're pregnant.'

She went behind the screen and got dressed while the doctor washed his hands.

'Pregnant,' she muttered in shock. She thanked the doctor and went out to her mother.

'Are you all right?' asked Ethel. 'You look a bit pale.'

'Mum, I'm pregnant,' said Rose, who was clearly still in shock.

'Come on, let's get you home,' replied Ethel as she headed for the door. 'We can talk about this when we get home.'

Once in Rose's flat Ethel made Rose lie down while she made some lunch.

'Well, are you happy about the baby?' asked Ethel as they ate.

'Yes, I'm just a bit shocked, that's all. I wonder how Stanley's going to take the news.'

'I'm sure he'll be over the moon,' Ethel said.

'I hope so,' replied Rose. 'Well, how do you feel, Grandma?'

'That is going to take a while to get used to, being called that,' Ethel laughed, 'me a granny. Rose, do you think you'll be all right here by yourself?' she asked seriously. 'What if you pass out here on your own?'

'I hadn't thought of that,' replied Rose worriedly.

'You could always come back home to stay if you like.'

Rose gave it some thought and said, 'Thanks, Mum, I'd like that,' Rose knew Stanley would be away for months yet and she didn't fancy staying alone in the flat on her own, in her condition.

That day Rose packed her case and went home with her mum. Once she had settled in she wrote to Stanley to tell him the good news, and got Freddie to post it for her. Rose continued working as a part time nanny until one day when she had got to three months she started to bleed. Helping Rose back into bed, Ethel sent for the doctor again.

Seeing Rose he said, 'You must rest in bed, you are not allowed to get out of bed for anything. Do you understand, Rose, you are at risk of having a miscarriage if you do,' he warned.

'What about if the sirens go off, what do we do then?' asked Ethel worriedly.

'Well, hopefully we won't have them but then if that happens she'll have to move.'

Ethel saw the doctor out and returned to Rose.

'Well, you heard him, you're not to move,' Ethel warned her; she knew what Rose was like, she would try and do things herself. 'I'll get your father to visit the Armstrongs and tell them you won't be able to look after their children.'

Rose did as she was told and sat in bed brooding about why she hadn't heard from Stanley; it had been months since she had written. Ethel tried to reassure Rose by saying, 'You know what the post's like, don't stress yourself out; it's no good for the baby.'

Stanley had been sitting on his bunk bed, shining his shoes, when the post had come. He went and got his letter and sat back down on his bed. He began to read.

'You got bad news from home, Stanley?' one of the lads said after he had seen Stanley's frown.

'Yes, you could say that,' he replied. 'My missus is pregnant.'

'I'd be over the moon if it was my missus,' said William, one of Stanley's mates.

'Well, it isn't your missus, so shut up,' barked Stanley as he screwed up the letter, threw it on the floor and stormed out of the barracks.

'Blimey, I feel sorry for his missus,' said one of the blokes, after Stanley had left.

William couldn't work him out. Stanley was so secretive all the time, he never talked about his wife or family; he acted like he had some dirty dark secret he had to keep.

Rose stayed at her parents' until they were sure she wouldn't miscarry, then she decided to go home to the flat. After being in bed for a month it felt good to walk around again. The following week Rose returned to work at the Armstrongs'; she had really missed the children.

'Guess what, Rose, we are going to boarding school full time next term,' said Oliver, the oldest one. 'So are we,' said the twins Sarah and Jessica, before they ran off to play hide and seek with her. Rose was upset; it was the first she'd heard about it. That night as Rose got ready to leave Mrs Armstrong called Rose into her study.

'Rose, can I have a word with you before you go.'

Rose went in and asked, 'Have I done anything wrong, Mrs Armstrong?'

'No, of course not, Rose, please sit down.'

Rose sat down and nervously played with the ring on her finger.

'I understand Oliver told you about the boarding school today.'

Rose nodded. 'Yes, he did.'

Mrs Armstrong looked flustered. 'We were going to tell you ourselves today; we decided it would be for the best if the children went now rather than later, especially after all the bombing going on around us at the moment.'

'I understand, when do you want me to go?' asked Rose sadly.

'Not until the end of the month, Rose.'

Rose left and got the bus home after speaking to Mrs Armstrong. She felt sad. She had looked after the children for almost all of their lives, seeing them take their first steps and their first words. Rose had seen them as family: what was she going to do now?

'You all right, Rose?' her mother asked as she walked into the house.

'Yes, I'm all right, thanks Mum.'

'What's wrong? You look like you've got the world on your shoulders.'

'I'm leaving my job at the end of the month. Mrs Armstrong is sending the children to boarding school full time,' replied Rose gloomily.

'Well, you would have left soon to have your own baby,' said Ethel.

'Yes, I know that, but I was hoping to go back afterwards,' Rose replied.

That night after returning to the flat Rose opened the door and saw a letter on the door mat. It had Stanley's handwriting scrawled all over the envelope. Reaching down she picked it up and ripped it open. She began to read. He had written asking her to send him some cigarettes and other items. He hadn't mentioned the baby or how she was; well, if he wanted to be like that he could forget about his cigarettes as far as she was concerned, he could go sing for them, she thought angrily.

The month flew by and on her last day at the Armstrongs' they surprised her with a cot for the baby. She was so overwhelmed she started to cry.

'Rose, don't cry,' said Sarah.

Rose hugged them all and thanked Mr and Mrs Armstrong for the present.

Getting into their car she was driven home. 'Well, take care, Rose, and don't forget you can still come and visit, the children and we would like that,' said Mr Armstrong as he took the cot up to the flat for her.

'Thank you, I will visit after I've had the baby,' replied Rose. 'Goodbye and thank you, Mr Armstrong.'

The last few months of Rose's pregnancy flew by and when Rose got to eight months she returned to her parents' to live.

'God, Mum, I look as big as a house,' she moaned as she tried to get out of the chair she had been sitting on. 'I can't even see my feet any more.'

Ethel thought she looked like a little round ball; Rose was tiny in stature.

'Never mind, love, you haven't got long now,' Ethel said as her knitting needles went ten to the dozen. She had been knitting baby clothes for months and was just finishing a matinee jacket.

'Did you hear what Freddie called me this morning, he said I was as big as a whale, the cheeky little sod. Lucky for him I wasn't quick enough to clip him around the ear. I must admit he is right. I feel like a beached whale,' said Rose. 'I just want it over with.'

A week before the due date Rose was sitting down knitting a baby blanket when she got a pain in her back. Rubbing it she said, 'I think I've been sitting down too long.'

'Maybe the baby's coming early,' replied Ethel.

'It's not due for another week.'

'Rose, they don't stick to a timetable, you know; they come when they are ready.'

'Mum, I got told the first one is normally late, I think I'll go and have a lay down,' Rose said as she tried to get out of the chair.

Helping Rose to her feet, Ethel said, 'That might be a good idea, I'll call you when dinner's ready.'

Rose went upstairs to her room and lay down on the bed. She drifted off to sleep only to be woken by a terrible pain. Surely this wasn't the start of the labour, was it? She waited a while to see if she had another contraction. She didn't want the embarrassment of finding out that they were just Braxton Hicks contractions after the midwife had been called out.

Rose felt another pain twenty minutes later.

'Rose, has it started?' Ethel asked as she saw her daughter flinch in pain.

'Yes, I think it has,' Rose yelled.

'How far apart are they?' asked Ethel.

'Every twenty minutes at the moment.'

'I'll get your father to go and get the midwife,' said Ethel as she hurried out of the room. Percy hadn't long come in from work when Ethel told him about Rose going into labour.

'I'll go and get her now,' Percy replied as he shot off down the road.

Ethel returned to Rose. 'Your dad has gone to get the midwife for you.'

Rose just nodded; she was in the middle of a contraction.

Ethel stood helplessly by. She had had four children but it was a bit different when it was someone else going through it. She'd never delivered a baby before and wasn't keen to learn now. Come on, Percy, where are you? thought Ethel, as Rose's contractions got quicker. Rose was ten minutes apart when Percy arrived back on his own.

Hearing the front door slam Ethel shouted down the stairs, 'Well, did you get her?'

'No, she's been caught up with another delivery; she said she'd get here as soon as possible.'

'Mum!' shouted Rose.

Ethel went back in to the bedroom.

'Is she here?' asked Rose.

'No, not yet, but she will be here soon,' said Ethel, trying not to panic Rose.

Rose started to cry. 'I can't do this any more, why can't it stop?'

'Rose you are doing really well, just try to keep calm,' said Ethel.

'That's easier said than done,' she hollered.

Two hours later the midwife arrived.

'How is she doing?' she asked Ethel as she entered the room.

'They are two minutes apart now,' replied Ethel, who was relieved to see the midwife.

'Right, Rose, I need to take a look. Rose, you are almost there; you can start to push soon, just pant for now.'

'I want to push now!' cried Rose.

'I can see its head!' cried Ethel.

'Keep pushing, Rose, you are almost there,' the midwife encouraged.

Rose gave a huge push.

'Rose, you must stop pushing for a minute; the baby's cord is wrapped around its neck, I have got to get it off,' said the midwife.

While Rose panted the midwife unwrapped the cord.

'You can push now,' she said.

Rose pushed and out popped the baby.

'Rose, it's a boy!' cried Ethel.

Rose was exhausted but managed to give a smile when she was handed her son.

Looking at him he was perfect. 'Are his legs all right?' she asked the midwife. She was worried about him having the same leg deformity that she had been born with.

'He is fine,' the midwife said, 'no problems at all, Rose. Well, I better be off, I have another delivery to make.'

Ethel saw her out and went to tell Percy he had a grandson.

'Does that mean I'm an uncle?' asked Freddie.

'Yes,' replied Percy.

Freddie laughed. 'I'm too young to be an uncle.' He was twelve years old.

'Is it all right to come in?' asked Percy.

'Yes, Dad, come and meet your grandson,' said Rose.

Percy went into the bedroom and sat on the edge of the bed.

'Well, what do you think?' asked Rose.

'He's a little smasher. What are you going to call him?'

'I thought of Tom Edward,' replied Rose.

'Can't I take a look at him?' called Freddie from outside the bedroom door.

''Course you can, you silly bugger,' said Rose.

'He's a bit small, ain't he?' Freddie said.

'Just as well he was,' replied Rose 'Sorry if I kept you awake.'

'That's all right, Sis, just don't do it again on a school night.'

Rose ruffled her brother's hair. 'Go on or you'll be late for school. You can't teach your new nephew bad tricks, I expect him to look up to you, you know.'

'Come on, let Rose get some rest; she was up all night, last night.'

Rose slept till late in the morning. She only woke up because her mother woke her to feed Tommy.

Rose wrote to Stanley to tell him he had got a son. She didn't expect a reply as he had made it obvious he didn't want to know about the baby or her, she thought miserably. She got Freddie to post it after he had finished school.

Two weeks after Tommy had been born Rose was in the garden hanging out some nappies she had washed. 'Mum, do you suppose he got the letter I wrote to him?'

'I don't know, love,' replied Ethel; she didn't know what to make of it.

'I guess he hasn't taken the news well; look how nasty he was when I wrote to him about the baby before he was born,' Rose replied sadly.

'Well, it's his loss,' said Ethel. Ethel was concerned. She knew Stanley didn't want to be a father, but it was a bit late for that now. It had crossed Ethel's mind that perhaps he would walk out on them but she never mentioned it to Rose; she didn't want to worry her needlessly.

Stanley had received Rose's letter and read it grimly. Damn, he thought. Now I'm stuck with her and another screaming brat to look after. He hadn't told Rose he'd got two children from a previous marriage. There was certainly a lot she didn't know about Stanley Noble.

Rose hadn't heard from Stanley for six months. All his letters had stopped when Tommy had been born and she hadn't received that many when he had found out about her pregnancy. She felt sad. This was meant to be a happy time of life but all she felt was numbness. She loved Tommy and couldn't understand why his father was so heartless.

Ethel was mystified by her son-in-law's behaviour. Why did he bother marrying Rose just to put her through all of this? How could he be so cold towards his own flesh and blood? she wondered.

One evening Rose had gone round to see her parents and had gone upstairs to get something. Percy and Ethel sat and discussed Stanley's behaviour.

'That bloke has got a lot of growing up to do,' said Percy angrily.

'Well, they have certainly got a lot of talking to do when he gets his next leave,' replied Ethel.

Rose had come down and had overheard her parents talking. She had sat on the stairs and listened to them, tears falling down her face. God, she felt miserable, how did things go so wrong?

Ethel carried on talking, unaware that Rose was listening, 'I wish Rose had never met bloody Stanley Noble, he's made her life hell.'

'Well, I feel sorry for that little boy, what sort of life is he going to have with a father like him?'

Rose had heard enough and coughed loudly to let on that she was coming back.

'You know what, you are both right about Stanley but what can I do?'

Ethel looked uncomfortable and looked at Percy; she hadn't realized Rose had heard. 'I'm sorry, Rose love, but you have to admit that since you married him you have been so miserable. Your Father and I hate seeing you like this.'

That night Rose returned home to the flat and had just put Tommy to bed when the siren went off. 'Not again,' she said aloud as she rushed to get Tommy and herself down to the shelter. Rose hated sitting in that old smelly thing with all the neighbours; it was so cramped and suffocating in there.

'You all right, Rose?' asked Vera, one of the neighbours.

'Yes, I'm just fed up today,' was her reply.

Vera knew better than to ask and left it at that. She knew what a bastard Rose's husband was and had heard him that night he'd hit her and they had rowed; the walls were paper thin and you couldn't help but hear. Changing the subject she said to Rose, 'Tommy has really grown, hasn't he?'

Rose smiled. She loved talking about her son. 'Yes, he has. He's six months old now, he'll be crawling soon.'

Just then there was a loud bang and the shelter rocked. 'Bloody hell, that was close; it must of been on the other side of the street by the sounds of it,' shouted one of the men in the shelter. They sat in the air raid shelter most of the night, Rose's back was aching from sitting in the same position and Tommy couldn't settle down, he kept crying.

'Poor little mite. Rose, give him here for a little while,' said Rita, her next door neighbour. Rose handed him to her and she tried to settle him.

'I hope my parents went into the shelter at the bottom of their garden,' said Rose. 'My mum doesn't always go; she'd rather go under the stairs and wait it out.'

'I'm sure your dad got her down there,' said Vera.

'Let's hope so,' Rose replied. She worried about her family more than she did about Stanley.

'You heard from your Joyce, Rose?' asked Rita.

'Yes she's coming home on leave soon.' Rose had got a letter from her saying she couldn't wait to see her nephew; she had only just gone back the week before Rose had Tommy and hadn't seen him yet.

The all clear sounded and they all wearily walked back to their homes. The sky was smoky from the fires that had been burning all night and the smell of acrid smoke made Rose feel sick; she got indoors as fast as she could.

That morning Ethel hurried along the road to visit Rose. She was worried as the bombs from the previous night had been raining down over near to where Rose lived. Ethel had heard from someone that the next street to where Rose lived had been flattened, so she had sat in the air raid shelter at the bottom of her garden worrying and waiting for the all clear.

'Mum, what are you doing here this time in the morning?'

'I had to make sure you and Tommy were all right; the next street down has been flattened.'

'Yes, I know, we heard it from the shelter. So many people have been made homeless through last night's bombing it makes you wonder where they will all go.'

'They will probably have to squeeze in with family,' said Ethel.

Chapter 8

Joyce came home on leave the following week and Rose was overjoyed to see her sister.

'Well, where is he then?' she asked as she came through the door.

'Well, that's a nice welcome home for your old mum,' teased Ethel. She knew Joyce couldn't wait to see Tommy.

'Oh Rose, he's lovely,' said Joyce. 'Can I hold him?'

Rose handed him to her and Joyce sat him on her lap and cooed at him.

'He likes you; normally he cries if he doesn't know you,' said Rose.

'Are you hungry, Joyce?' asked Ethel.

'I'm starving, Mum, it was such a long train journey and of course it was packed.'

Ethel returned with a plate of sandwiches and a pot of tea. 'Come on, put that baby down for a minute and come and get something to eat,' she laughed.

Joyce handed Tommy back to Rose and went and sat up at the table.

'What does Stanley think of Tommy?' Joyce asked. She hadn't heard about what had been going on with Stanley; Rose hadn't told her in her weekly letters.

'He hasn't seen him yet.'

Ethel gave Joyce a meaningful look, which she noticed and quickly changed the subject. 'So how are things up where you are?' asked Ethel.

'Not too bad. I hear you have had some nasty raids back here,' said Joyce.

'We have; the next street to me was flattened in the raid last week and twenty people were killed in just that street,' replied Rose.

'Oh my god,' said Joyce. 'I knew some people who lived there.'

'Bloody war, I'll be glad when it's finished, all these poor people killed for no reason at all,' said Ethel angrily.

They had a good day catching up with all the gossip and after dinner Rose took Tommy home.

'So what's happening with Stanley, then?' asked Joyce.

'I didn't want to say anything in front of Rose, it just upsets her,' said Ethel.

While they washed up the dishes Ethel told Joyce about the lack of enthusiasm Stanley had towards his son.

'I always thought he was a creep, the first night I set eyes on him,' said Joyce angrily.

'That's not all of it; he hit Rose a while ago, before she was pregnant.'

'The bastard, how come I wasn't told?' asked Joyce.

'Your dad didn't even know. Rose turned up here one night after a row and made me promise not to say anything to the family. Joyce, you must promise me not to say anything to your father about what I have just told you,' said Ethel.

'Okay, Mum, I promise I won't say anything to Dad.'

The following day, Joyce and Rose went for a walk with Tommy in his pram.

'Rose, what's going on with you and Stanley?'

Rose would have told anyone else who had asked her that question to mind their own business but with Joyce she could talk to her.

'Since Stanley found out about Tommy I haven't really heard from him. He wrote months ago asking me to send him some cigarettes, but I didn't bother, he didn't even ask about his own son,' said Rose bitterly.

'It sounds to me like he's jealous of Tommy,' replied Joyce. They had found a place to sit in the park away from the sun.

'How can a grown man be jealous of a baby?' Rose replied.

'I just know it happens, so have you written any more to him?'

'No, he knows where we are if he wants us,' Rose said defiantly.

It was obvious Rose wasn't happy but how could she help her sister, Joyce thought sadly.

'Joyce, I don't love him any more, I'm so unhappy.'

Joyce hugged her sister; there wasn't much more she could do. 'Come on, let's go home; it's almost dinner time and Mum won't appreciate us being late.'

The week was coming to an end and soon Joyce would have to go back to the Naval base up North. She spent as much time as she could with Rose, giving her a shoulder to cry on when she needed it. At the end of the week she left with a heavy heart. She wished she wasn't so far away.

Chapter 9

Rose insisted on seeing Joyce off at the station. She had brought Tommy along as well. As the train came in they hugged and kissed each other goodbye.

Joyce got on board the train and waved from the window until she could not see Rose any more.

Rose stood crying on the platform thinking, Why does everyone I love have to leave me? This damn war, I can't wait for it to finish.

Joyce reached the Naval base only to find out her best friend Peggy had been killed while she was away on leave; she was told the ship she had been on had been torpedoed and all hands on deck had perished. The ship had never made it to Malta. Joyce shuddered: she was meant to have been on that ship. She hoped poor Peggy hadn't suffered too much and hoped it had been quick. She had heard of sailors being attacked by sharks and hadn't wished that on anyone, least of all her friend.

One morning Rose had got back from shopping to discover Stanley waiting on the doorstep. She was angry. She hadn't heard from him for almost a year and his son was to have his first birthday soon, not that he cared.

'What the hell are you doing here?' she spat. 'You've got a bloody nerve turning up out of the blue like nothing has happened.'

'Well, that's a nice welcome home,' Stanley said.

'What do you expect, you never returned my letters.' Rose couldn't believe his cheek.

'How about a cuppa; I'm parched,' he said, changing the subject.

'You know where the kettle is,' Rose said.

Rose put her few items of shopping on the kitchen table, and took Tommy into the front room and sat him on the floor with his toys while she unpacked the shopping. Tommy started to cry. 'Well, are you going to pick your son up then?'

Stanley looked horrified and said, 'No way, he's your kid, not mine.'

Rose was furious, stormed into the front room and picked him up. 'I think you had better go,' she warned Stanley.

That was fair enough. He didn't want to be around a screaming brat and the old bat that Rose had turned into anyway. Stanley left and headed to the nearest pub he could find. He stayed there all day getting completely drunk until the barman in the hotel he visited kicked him out. 'Come on, son, on your way,' the barman said.

That night Stanley went back to the flat. Rose heard him outside the door and dragged him inside.

'Shush, you'll wake Tommy,' she said.

'I don't bloody care about Tommy,' he slurred.

'Well I do, so just shut up,' Rose said angrily. 'Well done, you've woken him up.' Rose went to get him.

'Shut that bloody thing up or I will,' he threatened.

'You'll do no such thing,' said Rose as she tried to calm Tommy. Rose was worried and tried to settle Tommy down; she knew what Stanley was capable of when he was drunk. Rose returned to the front room to discover Stanley in a drunken stupor in a chair. She felt relieved; at least he couldn't do anything while he was asleep. She went to bed herself and tried to get to sleep. She had a restless night tossing and turning, as she was wary of Stanley; she wasn't sure what he would do.

In the morning she got up early and dressed, and went

into the front room to see if Stanley was still there. He was – unfortunately, thought Rose. He was holding his head feeling sorry for himself.

'How do you feel?' asked Rose.

'How do you think I feel? I've got a bloody headache, you stupid cow,' he sneered.

Any sympathy she felt for him had gone; she wanted to get away from him as fast as she could. She dressed Tommy and said, 'I'm going out.'

'Do what the bloody hell you like,' he said.

'Don't worry, I will,' she threw back as she slammed the door.

'Hello, love, you're early,' said Ethel as Rose came into the house.

'I just had to get out of the flat. Stanley turned up yesterday after I got back from shopping. Do you know what, Mum, he hasn't half got a cheek.'

'What happened?'

'Nothing much. I gave him a piece of my mind and he left and went and got drunk.'

'He didn't hurt you, did he?' Ethel asked worriedly.

'No, when he came back he was so drunk he couldn't do anything, he fell asleep in the armchair, thank God.' Rose didn't trust him around her son and it worried her. What would he be like after the war ended? She knew she shouldn't think it but she hoped the war wouldn't end for years yet. She couldn't face living with him ever again.

'Rose, have you eaten yet?' her mother asked, interrupting her thoughts.

'No, we haven't. I just wanted to get out of his way.'

'Go and sit up the table. I'll go and make you and Tommy breakfast.'

Ethel cooked some eggs and buttered some bread. 'Here you go, eat up before your eggs get cold,' she said.

'Mum, do you mind if I stay all day?'

''Course you can love, I wouldn't mind the company,' replied Ethel.

Rose helped her mother out by doing some chores.

That evening the family where sitting down after their dinner when there was a loud knock on the door.

'Whoever can that be?' asked Ethel.

Rose had a good idea who it was; she knew it would be Stanley.

'I'll go,' said Percy.

'Where's Rose?' asked Stanley as he barged past Percy.

'Here, what's your game, barging into my home like that?' shouted Percy.

'Rose, you're coming home with me,' Stanley shouted as he grabbed her wrist and dragged her out of the room.

'Leave her alone!' shouted Ethel.

Percy stepped in and barred his way.

'Get out of my way or I'll thump you,' warned Stanley.

'Dad, it's all right, please let him through,' pleaded Rose; she didn't want her father getting hurt. 'Stanley, let go of my wrist,' she said calmly.

He let her go and stood glaring at Percy.

'Mum, would you look after Tommy for me tonight, please.'

'Yes, of course I will, love.'

'You don't have to go with him,' said Percy.

'Yes, she does, she's my wife!' shouted Stanley. Rose left with Stanley; she didn't want to but she didn't think that she had much choice.

They walked home in silence. Rose was glad she didn't have Tommy with her; God knows what Stanley would have done to him the mood he was in.

They got back to the flat and Stanley ordered Rose into the bedroom.

'No,' said Rose.

Smack his fist went into her face. She cried out in pain. 'Do as you're told,' he barked.

'No,' she defiantly said to him. Stanley went to hit her again.

'Go on then, do it, go on,' she shouted, 'hit me, show everyone what a coward you really are. You're only good at beating women, you're a bully.'

Stanley put his fists down. Rose went to walk past him to leave.

Stanley grabbed her and said, 'See how you like this, you bitch.' He grabbed her and pushed her onto the floor and ripped her dress as he tried to get her underwear off.

Rose screamed, 'No.' He covered her mouth with his hand and tried to pin her down so she couldn't struggle. Oh my god, he's going to rape me, thought Rose as she thought of how to get him off. She bit into his hand as hard as she could. It worked because he yelled in pain and let go, cursing at her. He looked at his hand: he'd got teeth marks in it. Rose made a run for the front door but he managed to beat her to it. 'Where do you think you're going?' he mocked as he blocked her exit.

'Don't come near me,' she cried, trying to put some distance between herself and him.

'You really think you're something special, don't you, you're just a snotty cow. You're lucky you have got me, no one else would put up with you' he sneered.

'If I had known I was marrying a drunken bully, I wouldn't have married you,' she spat back.

He went to hit her again. 'Go on, then, if it makes you feel like a man,' she mocked.

Rose was terrified but she stood her ground. She wasn't going to back down; she had her pride if nothing else.

He barged past her, he knew he had been beaten. He was going to get extremely drunk, he decided.

After he had left, Rose cautiously checked to make sure

he had gone. She slipped out of the flat and hurried along the dark streets towards her parents' home. She knew he'd be back later drunk and she wasn't going to stay and be his punch bag or worse. The streets were empty as Rose hurried along trying to keep her dignity as she held her dress together; he had ripped it up one side to the waist. Rose hadn't thought to grab her coat, she had just wanted to escape from him while she could.

Chapter 10

Stanley had headed to the nearest pub with more than hurt pride. He sat at the bar and ordered a drink. He still had Rose's teeth marks in his hand. The landlord of the pub noticed but didn't comment as he served him. Stanley sat nursing his third pint, thinking of ways he could get that bitch back. He came up with a plan and smiled to himself.

Rose walked along the road crying. She must have looked a state because a couple passed her and the woman asked if she was all right, did she need help?

Rose thanked her but said, 'No thank you, I'm all right,' as she hurried on.

The couple watched her as she walked away. 'Poor woman, I wonder what happened.'

'Come on, Elsie, if she didn't want help there is nothing we can do.'

'I guess not,' she said as she turned around and carried walking away.

Rose's bad leg was throbbing but she was too terrified to slow down; he could be following her, she thought. She kept looking behind imagining that he was about to jump out on her and was relieved to reach the end of Primrose Terrace: she was almost home. In the rush to get out she had forgotten her keys, so she hammered on the door until her father answered.

'Rose, what the hell happened?'

Rose pushed her father into the house and slammed the door shut. Crying on her father's shoulder she began to explain what happened.

Ethel heard the commotion and came into the hallway. 'Oh my God, Rose, are you all right?' She put her arms around Rose and took her into the front room. 'Sit down, love, you're shaking. Percy, go and make a cup of tea with plenty of sugar.'

Freddie had come down, he had been in bed. 'What's going on, Mum, what's wrong with our Rose?'

'Freddie, stop asking so many questions and get Rose a blanket,' Ethel said.

Freddie ran up the stairs, grabbed a blanket out of his bedroom and ran back down with it. 'Here you are, Mum.'

Ethel put it around Rose's shoulders and Percy came through with a cup of tea. 'Here you are, love, drink this.' He knew he wouldn't get anything out of her just yet; she was in shock.

'Freddie, get yourself off to bed,' said Percy.

'What's wrong with Rose, is she going to be all right?' asked Freddie.

'Yes, now go,' said Percy sternly. After Freddie had done as he was told Ethel asked Rose, 'Is this Stanley's doing?'

Rose nodded.

'I'll kill the bloody bastard,' Percy shouted.

Rose started to cry.

'Percy, you're not helping,' said Ethel. He sat down and kept quiet but he wanted Stanley's blood.'

'Rose, can you tell me what happened?' asked Ethel.

Rose said, 'We had a row and he hit me because I wouldn't do what he said.'

Ethel noticed the state of Rose's dress and said to Percy, 'Can you go and get me the antiseptic and cotton wool.' She wanted him out of the room while she asked Rose her next question. 'Rose, did he do anything else to you?'

'No, but he tried to. I managed to bite his hand, he let go then,' Rose started to cry again. Ethel was relieved: it wouldn't have been classed as rape in the eyes of the law but she was relieved that it hadn't happened for Rose's sake.

'Here you are, Ethel,' said Percy as he handed over the antiseptic.

'Rose, has he done this to you before?' asked Percy.

Ethel, who was cleaning her face, gave Rose a worried look.

'No, Dad,' she lied; she had seen her mother's worried face.

'I think you should leave him,' said Ethel, putting the lid back on the antiseptic.

'Mum, you know I can't, how would we survive without money?'

'You can come back here; we will support you and Tommy.'

Rose replied after a moment's hesitation, 'Thank you, Dad, but it will be all right; he's going to be gone soon again.'

'Well then, until he does you're staying here,' said Ethel sternly.

Rose stayed for a week, as she knew Stanley's leave was up by then. She went back to the flat with Percy who had insisted he was going with her just in case he was still there. Percy entered the flat first to check that it was okay to go in.

'Rose, you had better come and take a look.'

Rose entered the flat and cried in disbelief. The whole flat had been wrecked; everything had been smashed up. They went from room to room: everything had been broken, all the furniture and what had been there when she had moved in.

'Dad, look at this place,' said Rose sadly; he had even broken Tommy's cot. 'He's done this to get back at me; he knew it would hurt me more by doing this.'

Percy looked around. 'It looks like you'll lose your deposit now.'

'Oh my God, what am I going to tell Mr Smith, my landlord,' sobbed Rose.

'Come on, we will go and see him now,' said Percy.

Rose went down to his shop and after waiting for the customers to go she spoke to him.

'Rose, I have heard about the flat,' he said angrily.

'I have only just got back, my husband did it.'

'You know you'll lose the deposit, don't you, Rose.'

'What if we can replace what's broken?' asked Percy.

'Well, if you can do that, I might consider letting you off. You're lucky I never called the police, that's criminal damage, young lady.'

'It wasn't Rose's fault. It was that maniac she's married to,' said Percy defensively.

'I know it's none of my business, Rose, but I'd leave the bugger if I was you,' said Mr Smith.

It was agreed that if Rose could replace the broken furniture she could still have her deposit back when she eventually moved out. Mr Smith would have loved to have turned her out on her ear but after hearing Rose's side of the story, he was more sympathetic; it wasn't her fault she'd married a right bastard.

'Well, how am I going to replace the furniture then?' Rose asked, after they had left the shop.

'We will tell people that you had a flood and it had ruined all your stuff. We'll ask the neighbours, I'm sure they must have some bits spare,' replied Percy.

They went back to the flat and had a sort through to see what could and couldn't be repaired. After they had finished they went home.

'You took your time,' said Ethel crossly. 'Your dinner's ruined now.'

'Sorry, Mum, it was my fault we're late. Dad was helping

me tidy up. Stanley has gone and wrecked all the furniture in the flat, Tommy's cot, my table and chairs, everything. We saw Rita when we came out, she told me he had gone mad smashing everything up. She knew I wasn't there, she saw me leave after the row last week. She told me to leave the bastard, didn't she, Dad?'

Percy nodded.

'Well, I agree you should leave him, Rose, he has sunk to an all time low: just when you think there is nothing more he could do, he does this,' said Ethel.

'We still need to sort out what we're going to do about the furniture. Ethel, could you ask some of the neighbours if they have got anything spare they don't want,' asked Percy. 'I'll ask in work if any of the lads have got anything for Rose. We will tell everyone that Rose's pipes burst.'

'I'll go and ask Rene,' said Ethel. 'I won't be long,' she said as she hurried out of the door.

Everyone was glad to help and by the end of the week offers were flooding in. Rose had more than enough to refurnish the flat. Once Rose had finished she went and got Mr Smith so he could see the flat was back to normal.

After he had a good look around he said, 'Some of this stuff is better than what was here before. You can have your deposit back if you ever move out now, Rose.'

Rose thanked him and thanked her parents' neighbours with a box of fresh eggs she got from her grandparent's farm as appreciation. It wasn't much but Rose felt sure the eggs would come in useful especially considering they were hard to come by since the war. People had to use dried eggs which they moaned tasted vile.

Rose went back to the flat and her life got back to normal. She didn't hear any more from Stanley and she was glad. She hoped he would keep away for good.

Chapter 11

'That's strange, I haven't received my allowance in the post today,' Rose said to Ethel as she watched the postman go by her flat.

Ethel had got round Rose's early; they were going shopping and wanted to get first in line for the baker's opening.

'Maybe he hasn't been yet,' replied Ethel.

'Yes he has, he's been next door,' said Rose worriedly; she needed to go shopping as she was out of everything and needed to stock up again.

'Don't worry, I'm sure you'll get it, love,' said Ethel. 'If you like I'll lend you some money and you can pay me back when you've got it.'

'Thanks, Mum, but I can't borrow off you, you need it.'

'Here, Rose, take it. It's just a loan, you can pay me back when you've got it.' Ethel forced the money on to Rose.

'Thank you, Mum, I wouldn't be taking it but I'm desperate.'

They did their shopping and went back to the flat. Still nothing.

'Maybe it will come tomorrow,' said Ethel.

'Yes maybe,' said Rose worriedly.

The problem was it didn't come the next day or the day after that, either. Rose sat down and wrote to the Army to find out what was going on, and posted the letter that day.

Two weeks later Rose had gone to her mother's early one morning. There was a knock at the door and Rose went to answer it. She was shocked to discover two Army personnel officers standing on the doorstep.

'Hello, can I help you?'

'We are looking for a Rose Noble,' one of them said.

Rose's first thought was that Stanley had been killed. In a shaky voice she said, 'I'm Rose Noble, has something happened to my husband?'

'Can we come in, we need to talk to you about the letter you wrote to us.'

Relieved it wasn't Stanley, she let them in. Rose hated Stanley but didn't wish him dead. She led them into her mother's front room.

'How did you find me?' Rose asked. 'I had given my own address.'

'We knocked on your door and one of the neighbours gave us this address.'

Ethel came into the room. Startled by their presence she said, 'It's not George is it?'

Rose quickly explained why they were there.

Ethel was visibly relieved and made herself scarce in the kitchen.

'Mrs Noble, it appears that Private Stanley Noble is already married.'

'Yes, to me,' replied Rose.

The officer carried on: 'No, I am sorry to have to tell you but he was married before he married you.'

'No.'

Ethel came into the room. 'What's going on, Rose?'

'Mum, they are saying that Stanley was already married before he married me,' said Rose in a shocked voice.

'That can't be right, can it?' asked Ethel.

'Stanley Noble married his first wife in 1934,' said one of the Army personnel.

'No,' said Ethel as she sank into a chair. 'So what happens now?' she asked.

'He has been arrested and will be coming home to a Court Martial, where he will be dishonourably discharged.'

'Will Rose have to go to Court?' asked Ethel.

'Yes most likely,' one of them said.

Ethel saw them out and went to comfort Rose.

'Mum, how could he do this to me?'

Putting her arm around Rose she said. 'Look on the bright side at least you don't have to divorce him now, you're free of the monster.'

'That's true, Mum, but that means Tommy's illegitimate,' replied Rose.

Ethel hadn't thought of that; she was more concerned about her daughter.

'Let people think what they like,' said Ethel. 'We know the truth, that's all that matters.'

That night when Percy had got home from work, Ethel gingerly explained to him what had happened that day. Rose sat and listened while her dad sat stony faced and looking as if he was about to explode.

'I'll kill the bloody bastard,' Percy raged. 'How dare he make a mockery of our family like that?'

'Percy, calm down, you're not helping our Rose, can't you see how upset she is?' said Ethel sharply.

Rose ran out of the room sobbing; she felt embarrassed – how could she have been so stupid?

'See what you've done,' replied Ethel.

'I'll go and talk to her,' said Percy. He left the room and went upstairs and tapped on her bedroom door. 'Rose, can I come in?'

'Yes,' she said wiping her eyes on her sleeve.

'I'm sorry for shouting, I should never of taken it out on you.'

'Thanks, Dad, what am I going to do now? I haven't got any money coming in.'

'Don't worry about that, we'll take care of you and

Tommy,' replied Percy. 'Come on, love let's go downstairs; we have a lot to sort out.'

'Rose, what will you do, are you going to report Stanley?' asked Ethel as they sat around the table discussing what needed to be done.

'Yes, I'm going to the police station tomorrow,' said Rose. 'He has done more than enough to make my life miserable; it's about time I repaid the favour.'

'Do you want me to come with you?' Percy asked.

'Yes please, Dad.' Rose was relieved; she hadn't wanted to go on her own.

'Why don't you sleep on it for tonight and decide in the morning what you're going to do,' said Ethel.

The following morning Rose got up and said, 'I've decided to report him to the police, Dad, will you go with me still?'

'Yes, course I will. If you wait until I have finished work we can go then,' replied Percy. 'I think you are doing the right thing.'

'We are proud of you, you have had to make a hard decision,' said Ethel.

'Thanks, Mum.' Rose went and hugged her mum and dad. 'I don't know what I'd do without you both.'

Rose had got her marriage certificate out of the box she kept it in and stared at the worthless piece of paper. She wanted to rip it into tiny little pieces but instead threw it in her handbag and snapped it shut.

That evening Rose and her father went to the police station. Rose stood outside hesitating.

'Rose, are you sure you want to do this?'

'Yes, Dad, I was just getting a bit nervous, that's all.'

Percy opened the door and Rose entered. 'We would like to report a crime,' said Percy.

'Oh yes, and what was the crime you wish to report?' asked the desk Sergeant.

'Bigamy,' said Rose.

'If you would like to take a seat, I'll go and get someone,' replied the Sergeant.

'If you would come with me,' someone eventually said, and they were led into an interview room, which was a bleak looking place with just three chairs and a table.

Rose answered all of the questions and handed over her marriage certificate as evidence. She was glad to get it over and done with.

'Well done, love,' said Percy once they had got outside.

'Thank you for going with me, Dad, I couldn't have done it without you.'

They got home and Ethel asked, 'Well, how did it go?'

'They are looking in to it,' replied Percy as he sat down.

'We have just got to wait now,' said Rose.

Over a cup of tea plans were made about Rose's future. 'You had better move back here, Rose, you won't be able to keep the flat on any more,' said Percy.

Rose thought for a moment or two. 'The flat is paid up till the end of next week; I'll move back then if that's all right.'

That night Rose went to see Mavis. She knew what had happened and was disgusted to hear what Stanley had been up to. 'Well how did it go?'

Rose told Mavis and her mother what happened that day.

'What a nasty so and so. Rose, you're better off without him,' replied Mrs Jones.

Chapter 12

On the day Rose moved out of the flat, Percy and Freddie helped Rose; she didn't have much to take and they quickly loaded her stuff.

Rose had been to see Mr Smith the landlord and told him she was moving out. He hadn't been surprised by Rose's plan, as he had heard from Mrs Jones what had happened.

'Well, good luck, Rose, I hope everything turns out right for you.'

Rose went up to the flat and had a final look around. She had been happy here at first, she thought sadly to herself.

'Rose,' called Rita from outside the flat.

'Hello, Rita,' replied Rose.

'So it's true you are moving out, then?'

'Yes, Stanley won't be coming back.'

'Good, you deserve someone better than him,' replied Rita. 'So what happened, then?'

Rose chose her words carefully; she liked Rita but it was her business not anyone else's. 'Stanley has been captured and is in a prisoner of war camp so they think,' lied Rose.

'Oh, how awful,' replied Rita. 'I hope he is okay. Well, I must be going, take care of yourselves.'

'You okay, Rose, got everything,' asked Percy.

'Yes, Dad, let's go,' said Rose as she shut the door to the flat.

Rita knew Rose had lied to her but she could hardly blame her. At least she had the sense to leave the bastard, she thought as she rushed off to work.

Rose hated lying but she had to do it to protect her son; she knew how fickle people were.

'Hey, Ethel, what's your Rose doing back home?' asked Peggy.

'That's our business not yours,' said Ethel as she shook the breadcrumbs off the tablecloth and went back indoors. 'That bloody woman, why can't she mind her own business for once?' said Ethel angrily.

'Who are you on about, Mum?' asked Rose.

'That damn Peggy, all she does all day is gossip about people, hasn't she got anything better to do?' replied Ethel.

Rose knew the rumours had started about her and tried to stay in the house as much as she could to avoid them.

Peggy was like a dog with a bone; she was determined to find out what went on in the terrace they lived at. One morning Peggy caught Mavis as she was leaving her house. 'Here, Mavis, why's Rose living back at her parents'?' she asked as she stood at her front gate.

'I don't know, why don't you ask her yourself?' said Mavis as she hurried up the road to get away from the nosey cow.

'You stuck up old cow,' shouted Peggy, she suspected Mavis knew about Rose. Just then her neighbour Doris came out. 'Who was you shouting at?'

Doris was just as bad as Peggy; they made it their business to know what went on.

'That bloody Mavis, snooty cow, I only asked her why Rose was home again.'

'What did she say?' asked Doris.

'Nothing,' said Peggy.

That night after work Mavis went and knocked on number twelve to see Rose.

'Rose, I thought I'd better warn you Peggy's asking a lot of questions. This morning she collared me, she wanted to know why you were living back here.'

Rose had made a pot of tea and they were sitting in the

front room chatting, while Tommy played with his toys on the floor.

'I can't blame people, it must seem strange me coming back home after all this time,' replied Rose. 'So what are the rumours so far, then?'

'Well, some are saying you're widowed, others are saying he's left you for another woman.'

'Well, they have almost got the last one right,' replied Rose bitterly. 'You didn't say anything to Peggy, did you, Mavis?'

'Of course not,' she replied. 'I'd never do that.'

Rose told Mavis almost everything: the beatings, the fact that Stanley had never taken to his own son and the bigamy.

Changing the subject, Rose asked, 'Do you think the real Mrs Noble knows about me?'

'She probably does know now, but it isn't your fault, so stop beating yourself up over it,' said Mavis.

'Thanks, Mav,' replied Rose.

'I'd better go. I said that I'd help Mum with the dinner. Rose, promise me you'll remember what I said.'

Rose promised and saw her to the door.

Ethel came into the room and said, 'Has Mavis gone?'

'Yes,' Rose replied.

'You seem a bit happier than you did earlier. Mavis is a good friend, you need that right now,' said Ethel.

Mavis and Rose had been friends since they were tiny; they had been through an awful lot together and supported each other through times of need. Rose couldn't ask for a better friend.

'Good morning, is Rose Brown home?' asked the Police Constable.

'Yes, come in, Constable,' said Ethel. She hoped for Rose's sake he hadn't been seen knocking on their door.

Ethel shouted, 'Rose there is someone to see you.'

Rose came down the stairs and was shocked to see the policeman standing there.

Regaining her composure, she said, 'I'm Rose, how can I help?'

'Morning, Miss, I was sent to inform you that Stanley Noble has been arrested and he will appear in Court when a day has been set. You will be called as a witness.'

After seeing the Constable out Rose said, 'He's been arrested.'

'It couldn't have happened to a nicer bloke,' said Ethel as she went back to peeling the spuds. That night Rose told her father about the visitor that day.

'Well, I'm glad to see justice is being done,' he replied soberly.

'Well, I've probably given Peggy some juicy gossip,' replied Rose.

She was right, Peggy was in her element.

'Here, Doris, did you see that copper go in to the Browns'?' she asked.

'Yes, I did. I wonder if it's got to do with Rose's old man. 'Ere, you don't reckon he's been killed, do yer?' asked Doris.

'Don't be stupid, you get a telegram if it was that,' replied Peggy. 'No, there is something fishy going on there, mark my words.'

'Besides, you wouldn't keep that quiet, would you, you'd want the whole bloody world to know what a bloody hero he was,' said Peggy.

Rose was overjoyed to hear that Joyce was coming home on leave again, Rose hadn't seen her for six months and although they wrote every week it just wasn't the same. Rose had to admit she was worried that she was going to get one of Joyce's famous lectures. Sometimes she felt like she was the youngest of the two and she was six years older than Joyce.

'Well, how is my little nephew?' asked Joyce after she had greeted everyone.

'Oh Rose, he has really grown since I last saw him. Can he walk yet?'

'Yes, he took four steps the other day,' Rose said proudly.

Joyce picked Tommy up and sat him on her knee. He was holding a rattle in his podgy little hand and was trying to eat it.

Ethel came into the room with a tray of tea and a plateful of sandwiches for everyone, 'Here you are, tuck in, Joyce, I'm sure it has been a long time since you ate.'

'Thanks, Mum, these are lovely,' said Joyce. 'So Rose, have you heard when the court case is?'

'No, a date hasn't been arranged yet. I'm glad he has been arrested though.'

'It's bloody disgusting what he has done, I hope he gets the book thrown at him. Does our George know about Stanley?' asked Joyce.

'Yes, he wrote back saying he should be on leave soon,' replied Rose.

Rose hoped Joyce wasn't going to go on about Stanley; she was only home for a week and they had better things to discuss.

'Do you think he's got bail?' asked Ethel to Joyce after lunch. Rose had put Tommy to bed for his nap.

'Probably,' said Joyce.

'Well, I hope he stays away from our Rose,' said Ethel worriedly.

'Mum, don't mention that to Rose, you will only scare her,' warned Joyce.

'Don't mention what?' asked Rose as she came back into the room.

'Oh, nothing, love,' replied Ethel.

Rose didn't push it further; she knew it was about herself.

'Rose, when you hear about the date will you let me know so I can try and get leave?' asked Joyce.

'Yes, okay, but let's not talk about him anymore. I'm sick of hearing about him,' Rose replied sternly.

The week went far too quickly and soon it was time for Joyce to go back. They had had a lot of fun together; they had gone shopping and went for walks with Tommy and they had talked which had done Rose the world of good.

'Here is my train,' said Joyce as it came puffing into the station and stopped. Joyce kissed Tommy and handed him back to Rose. 'Take care of this one and take care of yourself, Rose,' said Joyce as she hugged and kissed her sister.

Joyce boarded the train and stood waving out of the carriage window. Rose waved back until she couldn't see her any more and then pushed Tommy home.

Rose had just got in when Ethel said excitedly, 'Guess what, George is coming home next week.' Ethel was thrilled. She hadn't seen her son for almost a year as his last leave had been cancelled. He always tried to get leave at the same time as Joyce if he could.

A week later George came home. He dumped his kitbag in the hallway and hugged his mother and Rose.

'How are you both?' he asked.

'Just fine, seeing you home safe and sound,' cried Ethel.

'It's great to be home again, I've really missed the place,' said George. 'Rose, I'm sorry to hear about your news. I wish I had been here: I'd have knocked his bloody block off,' he said angrily.

'It doesn't matter, you're here now,' replied Rose. 'Would you like to see your nephew?'

Rose took him upstairs to see Tommy. 'He has got your nose, the poor little bugger,' joked George.

Rose thumped him on the arm. 'Thanks a lot,' she

laughed. 'He has got the Browns' ears; he must take after you,' she joked.

That night there was a knock on the door and Percy got up to answer it.

'What the bloody hell are you doing here? You've got a nerve showing your face around here!' shouted Percy.

'Who is it, Dad?' asked Rose. She gasped when she saw who it was. 'What do you want?' she asked angrily. 'Don't you think you've done enough?'

'I want the jewellery back that I gave you,' he shouted.

George came to the front door. He'd been outside in the garden having a smoke.

'Is that Stanley?'

'Yes,' replied Percy barring the doorway.

'You can't have it,' yelled Rose. 'I pawned it,' she lied.

'You get lost,' shouted George, 'or I'll punch your face in,' he said angrily.

'Go on, then, if you're man enough,' sneered Stanley.

George stormed over to him and punched him in the face, sending Stanley flying.

'You haven't got such a smug face now have you?' shouted George. 'Go on, get lost and if I ever see you around my sister again I'll kill you.'

Stanley got up and as he walked away shouted, 'I haven't finished with you.'

As Stanley walked away all of the neighbours cheered; they had come out after hearing all the commotion and wanted to see what was going on.

'Come on, everyone, in now,' said Ethel; they had given the neighbours enough gossip for now.

'I can't believe he got bail,' said Rose.

'Was you really married to that creep?' said George. He hadn't met Stanley before.

'Yes, I was, well thought I was until recently,' said Rose.

'I doubt that he'll come back now,' replied George.

'I'll make damn sure of that,' said Percy. 'He must have broken his bail conditions. I'm going down the Police station tomorrow to let them know.'

Seeing Stanley had set her nerves off again, and Rose started to shake. Ethel noticed and went and made her a cup of tea with plenty of sugar.

'Here, love, drink this,' she said, placing it in Rose's hands. After a little while Rose felt okay again.

Freddie had been watching his big brother from the front window and was excited at what George had done. 'Cor, you were brilliant,' he said.

The next day Percy set off for the police station and reported Stanley to the police, who took it very seriously: he had been warned not to go near Rose or any of the family. He was arrested and sent to jail on remand.

'Come on, Sis, you can tell me what has been going on since I have been away.' George had persuaded Rose to go for a walk with him. She had refused at first as she felt sure Stanley was going to reappear and felt terrified of going out just in case he did. In the end they went for a short walk and Rose nervously kept looking around. They sat down and Rose told George everything that had happened since she had married that man.

'God, Rose, what a bastard,' said George, shaking his head. 'I wish I had been here.'

'You were, last night. I'm glad because he would have hurt Mum or Dad,' Rose said miserably.

A month later Rose received an official looking letter. She knew what it was and her heart sank. She had guessed right: it was the date for the court case and the date had been arranged for 11 August 1943 at 9 a.m. Rose had been dreading this day for months.

'Mum, it's here,' said Rose, showing her the letter.

Ethel read it and said, 'Don't worry, love, we will be there with you.'

Rose was grateful but she was the one giving evidence, she thought miserably.

That night Percy read it and said, 'I suppose I had better tell my mother before she hears it from someone else. I will go on Saturday.'

Saturday came and Percy walked to his parents' farm, which was a couple of miles away. He reached the farmhouse, tapped on the door and went in.

'Hello, son, what brings you here on your own?' asked Charlie.

'I've got some bad news, Dad.'

'It ain't George is it?' His father looked concerned.

'No, Dad, it's about our Rose,' replied Percy.

'I think we could do with a drink,' said Charlie as he poured a large Jack Daniels into two glasses and handed one to Percy.

'So what is it, son?'

'Rose has got to go to court in August. It turns out that Stanley was already married before he married our Rose.'

'Bloody hell, sneaky little bastard,' Charlie said.

'So where is Mother?' asked Percy.

'She's gone out on Star, she should be back soon, son.'

'I'll wait for her to come back then,' Percy replied. He was nervous. His mother was a hard old bat, who was like an exploding time bomb if she got angry.

'Do you want a bit of Dutch courage,' asked Charlie; he was aware of how his wife would react to this news.

Just then they heard a horse's hooves on the cobbled yard; she had come back. Percy went out to meet her.

'What are you doing here?' Jane asked sternly.

Helping her off the horse, he said, 'I've got some news you're not going to like.'

'Well, spit it out,' his mother said impatiently as she took the saddle off the horse.

Percy stood patting the horse and said, 'It's about our Rose.'

'What about her?' Jane asked.

'I'll tell you inside, Mother,' replied Percy.

Jane walked Star back to his stable and gave him a feed bag and walked up to the farmhouse with Percy. The atmosphere was always icy between them now. She had wanted Percy to marry a girl she had picked as a wife, but Percy had refused and had married Ethel, his childhood sweetheart, much to his mother's fury.

Once in the house Percy explained to his mother what he had explained to his father.

'What!' shouted Jane. 'She has brought shame onto this family, she has given birth to a bastard!' she roared.

'Jane,' said Charlie, 'she wasn't to know, leave the poor girl alone.'

'I think I had better go before I say something I'll regret,' said Percy.

Charlie saw him to the door and said, 'Let her calm down, son.'

Percy said goodbye to his father and walked home. As soon as he got through the door Ethel asked, 'Well, did you tell them?'

'Yes, I told them all right. Dad took it well but Mother hit the roof.' He wasn't going to tell them exactly what his mother said.

'I knew she would, it's no wonder she blamed me for raising Rose all wrong, I wouldn't put it past her,' moaned Ethel.

'No, she didn't blame you, Ethel,' Percy said crossly; he knew once they got onto the subject of his mother, Ethel would never shut up and he had had enough for one day.

'I'll go and cook the dinner then,' said Ethel; she knew by Percy's tone that she had hit a raw nerve.

Later that afternoon Rose came home with Tommy. They

had spent the day with Mavis and Rose was in a good mood for once. Rose went into the kitchen to say hello to Ethel and immediately noticed her mother was upset. 'Everything all right, Mum?' she asked.

'Yes, love,' Ethel answered.

'Have you and Dad had words?'

Ethel nodded as she carried on peeling the vegetables. 'Your dad went down to the farm this morning,' said Ethel.

'Oh, don't tell me, Grandma Brown, what has she done now,' asked Rose.

'You'd have to ask your father that,' she sniffed.

Rose hated her parents rowing; it was always about her grandmother.

'Hello, Dad,' said Rose as she went into the front room.

'Hello, love,' he said tiredly.

Placing Tommy on her father's lap she said, 'Someone missed you today.'

Percy smiled as he held his grandson on his lap.

'I hear you went to see Grandma today,' Rose said.

Percy's smile faded. 'Yes, I did.'

'I take it she didn't take my news well then?' asked Rose.

'No, she didn't, but it's nothing you need to worry about,' he said wearily.

'Have you and Mum had words again? She's really upset, Dad.'

'Your mother gets on her high horse every time I mention your grandmother,' replied Percy.

'You can hardly blame her, Dad, she is always criticising Mum,' Rose said.

'Rose, leave it, I have had enough for one day.' He handed Tommy back to her, grabbed his cap and coat, slammed the door and walked to the Fox and Hounds for some peace and quiet.

Ethel came into the room. 'Was that your father just now?' she asked Rose.

'Yes, Mum, I think Grandma gave him a hard time over me.'

'What did he say?' asked Ethel.

'Nothing, he didn't want to talk about it.'

Ethel felt ashamed; she knew Percy had a lot to contend with without her putting her foot in it as well.

'Rose, give me a hand, love, can you set the table and give Freddie a shout that dinner's almost ready.'

'What about Dad, do you want me to get him?'

'No, leave him, Rose, I'll put his in the oven,' Ethel replied.

Dinner was a quiet affair that night. Freddie could sense that something was wrong but had no idea why. 'Where's Dad?' he asked.

'Your father had to go out,' replied Ethel. 'Eat your dinner before it gets cold.'

Freddie ate his dinner quickly and asked to be excused. 'Mum, can I go back outside?' he asked.

'Yes, but make sure you are back before it gets dark, do you hear me?'

'Yes, Mum,' he said as he ran out of the house, slamming the door shut behind him.

'Sorry, Mum, it's my fault you and Dad had a row,' said Rose miserably.

'It's not your fault; if it's anyone's it's that grandmother of yours,' replied Ethel.

Rose didn't reply; she knew talking about her grandmother was like waving a red rag to a bull. Her mother and grandmother hated each other. Ethel knew her mother-in-law thought that she wasn't good enough for her precious son.

A few days later Rose's Uncle Jack came round.

'Hello, Rose, love,' he said as he hobbled into the house. 'Your dad home from work yet?'

'No, he should be home soon; would you like a cup of tea?'

'That would be grand,' he said taking the weight off his leg as he sat down in an armchair.

Rose loved her Uncle Jack. She had something in common with him, as he had a crippled leg as well except his had been from an accident. One day he had been out riding his favourite horse Flame when unexpectedly the horse was spooked by something and had reared up and galloped away with him clinging on for dear life until he could hold on no more and fell off into a threshing machine that was working in one of the top fields. The machine severed his left leg below the knee. He suffered other injuries as well but his leg was the worst. Rose's father had said that he was lucky to be alive. Granddad Charlie had heard the screams and had found him mangled in the machinery. That was something Charlie would never forget as long as he lived.

Jack had been twenty-one years old and had just been served his drafting papers for the Army during the First World War. He had wanted to serve his Country like his big brother Percy had, but Percy had thought at the time it was probably a blessing in disguise.

'Here you are, Uncle Jack,' said Rose, giving him his tea.

'Thank you, love, where is everybody?' he asked.

'Mum's at her friend's and Freddie is out playing with his friends.'

'I'm glad it's quiet. I wanted a word with you anyway. I heard about what Stanley did.'

'Oh,' said Rose; she felt ashamed.

'Don't worry, love, we are all on your side,' said Jack.

'What, even Grandma?'

'Your grandmother will come around eventually, just give her time,' Jack reassured her.

'Thank you, Uncle Jack.'

'So where is that handsome little boy of yours, then?' he asked.

'He's asleep at the moment.' Just as she said it Tommy started to cry.

'I'll just go and get him,' said Rose.

'Hello, son,' Jack said as he took him from Rose. 'My, you've grown,' he said, sitting him on his knee.

Just then Percy came home. 'Hello, Jack, how are you?'

'Not bad, you?' he asked. 'I just came round to have a chat with Rose.'

'Rose, where is your mother?' asked Percy.

'At Rene's, Dad, do you want me to go and get her?' she asked.

'Yes, go and get her and tell her we have got a visitor and he's staying for dinner, would you, love.'

Rose went to get her mother and left them to talk.

'It's bloody terrible what that bloody bloke did to your Rose,' said Jack as he shook his head.

'The bloody bastard knocked here a few weeks ago. Our George was home on leave and he hit him and sent him packing,' replied Percy, laughing.

'I hear Mother didn't take it too well,' Jack asked.

'No, she didn't, she was acting like Rose had deliberately done it to ruin our good name,' Percy said bitterly.

'She'll never change,' said Jack. 'She hasn't been the same since young Fred died from diptheria.' Ethel and Percy had named Freddie after him; he had died at thirteen years old and Percy and Jack's mother had never been the same since; she had become bitter and twisted.

'More's the pity,' said Percy. 'It's a shame that you have to put up with it.'

Jack had stayed living on the farm. Percy had been telling him for years to leave.

'Hello, Jack, how are you?' asked Ethel as she came in.

'Same as usual,' Jack replied.

Ethel was fond of her husband's brother; he had always treated her kindly even if his mother hadn't.

Ethel and Rose made the dinner and spent an enjoyable evening chatting with Jack.

Freddie was buzzing around like a blowfly. He never lost interest in Uncle Jack's exaggerated stories.

'Well, I had better go,' said Jack. 'It's late and I need to let you good people get to bed.'

Percy saw his brother to the door.

'Now, Rose, don't forget what I said,' said Jack as he left.

'I won't, I promise,' replied Rose.

Chapter 13

'Rose, are you ready?' Percy shouted. 'We have got to go, now.'

Rose was sitting on her bed trying to forget about this moment. It was the day of the Court case and she didn't relish facing Stanley again. Stanley had refused to admit guilt, much to Rose's disgust.

Sighing, Rose went downstairs and got into the car. Tommy had gone to Mavis's while she attended Court.

Ethel gave Rose's hand a squeeze and asked, 'You all right, love?'

'Yes, fine, I just want this over and done with.'

They reached the Old Bailey and stood outside the courtroom waiting for the case to begin.

'Rose, do you know that woman over there?' asked Joyce.

'What one?'

'The one in the blue dress,' replied Joyce.

Rose looked and said, 'No, I don't know her.'

'She keeps staring at you,' said Joyce.

'You don't reckon she's Stanley's real wife, do you?' asked Rose.

Their barrister hurried over to them and said, 'It's time to go in. Rose, I'm afraid because you're our first witness you will have to wait here.'

Percy, Ethel and Joyce wished her luck and went to take their seats.

Rose noticed the woman who had been staring at her was also waiting outside; it dawned on Rose that she must be the real wife after all. They didn't say anything to each other but just stared, weighing each other up.

In the Courtroom Stanley was brought up from the cells and asked, 'How do you plead, guilty or not guilty?'

'Not guilty,' he said in a loud voice.

There were moans coming from the galleries. 'Quiet in Court,' the Judge said, banging his gavel down to get everyone's attention. The muttering stopped and the case began.

Rose was called as the first witness. She took the stand and was sworn in and gave her name and address. She was so nervous, her knees were like jelly.

'When you met my client did you ask if he was married?' Stanley's barrister asked.

'Yes, I did ask him the first night we met; he told me he wasn't married,' replied Rose.

'You got married at St Mary's Church in Chingford on 18 May 1942, did you not?'

'Yes, that is right,' replied Rose.

The Judge was handed Rose's marriage certificate as evidence.

'Rose, isn't it true you forced my client into marrying you because you said you were in the family way?' asked Stanley's barrister.

'No, that is not true,' said Rose. 'I had my son nine months after we were first married.'

Rose began to feel as if she was the criminal.

Rose's own barrister started to ask her questions. 'Rose, did you believe Stanley Noble when he said he wasn't married?' asked Mr Gregory.

'Yes, I did believe him, why shouldn't I have?'

'Rose, how did you find out about Stanley being married?' asked Mr Gregory.

'My money from the Army was stopped so I wrote to them to find out why.'

'What happened then?' asked Mr Gregory.

'I had two Army personnel come to visit me.'

'And that is how you found out about your marriage being illegal,' said Mr Gregory.

'Yes, that is right,' replied Rose.

'No more questions, my Lord,' her barrister replied.

'You may sit down now, Miss Brown,' the Judge said.

Rose was relieved to get down, and return to her family.

The murmuring started in the Courtroom and the Judge shouted, 'Quiet in Court, any more noise and the Court will be cleared,' he said angrily.

The next witness was called and sworn in and gave her name: Elizabeth Noble, of 29 Wintergreen Terrace, Wanstead.

'How long have you been married to Stanley Noble?' asked Mr Gregory.

'Ten years,' she replied.

'When exactly did you get married?'

'April 24 1932' she said.

'Where did you get married?' asked Mr Gregory.

'At Wanstead Registry Office,' replied Elizabeth Noble.

'My Lord, I have got the documentation here to confirm this.' The barrister handed it over to a Court Clerk who took it over to the Judge to examine.

'Are there any more witnesses?' the Judge asked.

Both sides said, 'No my Lord.'

'Stanley Edward Noble, do you have anything to add?' asked the Judge.

'No, your Honour.'

'In that case we will adjourn for lunch and return at 1 p.m.,' replied the Judge.

'All rise!' the Court Usher shouted.

Stanley was led down to the cells and Rose and her family filed out into the corridor.

'I'm parched,' said Percy. 'Let's get something to drink.' They headed to the canteen and bought lunch.

'Well done, Rose, you did really well,' said Ethel.

'I was terrified; do you think he will get off?' asked Rose.

'It doesn't look that way. He hasn't got much of a case,' replied Percy.

'He couldn't even look me in the eye,' replied Rose.

'I hope he gets what he deserves,' said Joyce, much too loudly, to Ethel's embarrassment.

'Joyce, not so loud,' her mother warned.

'I don't care, Mum,' she said back loudly.

'Come on, it's almost time to go back,' said Percy.

They headed back to the Courtroom and waited in the corridor.

'How much longer do we have to wait?' asked Rose impatiently.

A little while later the court came back in to session and the Judge returned.

'All rise!' They all stood.

Everyone took their seats and waited for the verdict. The Judge addressed Stanley who had been brought back up from the cells.

'Stanley Edward Noble, you have been found guilty. I am sentencing you to seven years in prison which shall be carried out immediately. You have lied to the Army and to these unfortunate women. You have deceived them for your own perverted reasons, so I am giving you the fullest sentence possible for this crime.'

Rose stared at Stanley, he looked so pathetic. What had she seen in him in the first place? she thought as she watched him being led away.

'Court dismissed,' the Judge said.

'Rose, you've won,' shouted Joyce.

The cheering was unbelievable coming from the galleries.

Rose went over to thank Mr Gregory, her barrister, and

then they all filed out into the corridor. As Rose left she noticed Elizabeth Noble sobbing in the corridor, while people pushed and shoved to get out of the Courthouse. Rose felt sorry for her. 'Wait a minute, there is something I must do,' shouted Rose above the din of people's voices.

'What is she doing?' asked Joyce as she watched her walk over to Elizabeth Noble.

Rose handed her a handkerchief. 'Here, I think you need this,' she said.

'Thank you,' she said as she looked up and took the hanky.

'It looks like he fooled us good and proper,' said Rose.

'I know,' Elizabeth replied as she handed Rose's hanky back.

'No, you keep it,' said Rose. 'So what do you think you'll do now?'

'I'm not sure. I'm thinking of divorcing him.'

'Well, good luck, I hope you find happiness,' replied Rose as she walked away.

'Why did you talk to her?' asked Joyce angrily. 'It's not like she got the raw deal.'

'I think you will find she was just as much a victim as I was; he betrayed her more than me,' said Rose as they left the Courthouse.

'Well, I think you were very good for being so compassionate, not many people would have done what you did,' said Ethel.

'Come on, let's go home and celebrate,' said Percy.

They came down the steps of the Courthouse and were surrounded by reporters.

Rose was being asked questions as Percy tried to get her to the car.

'No comment,' he shouted angrily. They got to the car and all quickly got in.

'Bloody reporters,' said Percy as he drove away.

'Don't say they are going to write about me,' said Rose. 'That's all I need.'

'We will have to wait and see,' said Ethel. She hoped for Rose's sake they wouldn't.

Rose went to collect Tommy from Mavis's.

'Well, how did it go?' she asked.

'He got seven years,' said Rose.

'You don't seem too happy about it,' replied Mavis.

'I am, it's just that as we left Court there were loads of reporters asking me lots of questions. What if they put it in the papers, I'll die of shame. So how has Tommy been?'

'He's been a bit grizzly, I think he missed you.'

Rose took him and said, 'It's probably a tooth coming through. Thanks for looking after him for me, I'll see you tomorrow.'

'Rose, come on, grab a drink,' said Percy. 'Here's to a new future.'

'Cheers.'

Rose was relieved that it was all over at last; she was rid of Stanley Noble and she hoped she never saw him again.

Chapter 14

Percy had got up early the next morning and had gone and bought a newspaper.

'Here, Percy, there's a bit in here about your Rose,' said the newsagent.

Percy paid for it and rushed home to read it. 'I don't bloody believe it, Ethel, come and have a look.' They both read the article about Rose.

'How could they do this?' said Ethel angrily.

'Bloody reporters, anything for a good story. They would sell their own mothers if they could,' said Percy.

'Quick, hide it, Rose is coming,' said Ethel urgently.

Percy stuffed it under the chair cushion and sat on it.

'Mum, have you seen Tommy's other shoe? I need it, I'm going to take him shopping with me.'

'Rose, why don't I come with you, I could do with some fresh air.' They hunted for the shoe and got ready to leave.

'Not much here,' moaned Rose as they looked around the shops in the High Street.

'Mum, is it me or am I getting funny looks?' asked Rose.

'No, I haven't noticed anything,' lied Ethel.

'I had better go into the newsagent's. I'm almost out of envelopes,' said Rose.

Ethel was horrified. 'No, leave it, Rose, I have got some at home you could have.'

Much to Ethel's relief Rose agreed to have some of hers.

They were heading home when Rose said, 'Hello,' to two women she had been to school with.

'I'm surprised you're showing your face around here,' one of them said.

'What do they mean by that?' asked Rose after they had walked away.

'I don't know; come on, let's get home. I'm gasping for a cuppa,' said Ethel, trying to change the conversation.

They had just reached the end of the terrace when Peggy shouted out, 'Oh look, if it isn't the snotty cow with her bastard son.'

Rose spun round. 'What did you call me?'

'You heard,' she said. 'Not so high and mighty now, are we?'

'Rose, come on,' said Ethel as she pulled her away.

'Go in, Peggy,' shouted Ethel. 'Before I do something un-ladylike.'

Once inside Rose raged. 'How the hell did she know, Mavis is the only one outside this family that knows, she hadn't better of said anything.'

'Rose, sit down, there is something I want you to read.' Ethel pulled out the newspaper and gave it to her. 'We tried to keep this from you, we knew it would upset you again; look at page 3.'

Rose read the article about herself in the local *Herald* and threw it on the floor. 'How could they do this to me?' she sobbed.

'Just give it a few days; it will soon blow over,' said Ethel.

'Chance would be a fine thing,' Rose replied miserably.

A week after the trial had finished there was a knock at the front door. Wondering to herself who that could be Ethel went to answer it. She opened the door and standing on the doorstep were a man and woman impeccably dressed.

'Can I help you?'

'Yes, could you tell us if Rose Brown lives here, please?' asked the woman.

'Who wants to know?' asked Ethel suspiciously.

'We are Stanley's parents,' said the man.

'You can't be, he didn't have any that were alive,' said Ethel.

'Please let us come in to see Rose; we will explain everything,' said the woman desperately.

'Wait here, I will see if Rose will see you,' said Ethel. 'Rose, there are some people at the door saying they are Stanley's parents.'

'No, they can't be,' said Rose.

'Give Tommy here and go see what they want,' said Ethel.

'Hello, can I help you?' Rose asked. She was shocked: the man was the image of Stanley but much older.

'Rose, can we come in and talk to you?' asked the woman.

Rose led them into the front room. 'Please sit down,' she said. 'Stanley told me you died in an accident years ago.'

'How could he say such a thing?' the woman sobbed.

'Well I'm hardly surprised by it,' said the man. 'Let me introduce ourselves: this is Diana and I am George Noble. We fell out with Stanley eight years ago and haven't heard or seen him since,' said George.

'Rose, is everything all right?' asked Ethel as she entered the room.

'Yes, Mum,' replied Rose.

The couple explained what had happened and Ethel said, 'Pardon me for being rude. Rose has been hounded by the press and they have tried almost everything to talk to her.'

'We can understand that,' said Diana.

'Would you care for a cup of tea?' asked Ethel.

'Thank you, that would be lovely,' replied Diana.

Ethel went out to make the tea; she got her best cups and saucers out and boiled the kettle.

'So why did you fall out with Stanley, if you don't mind my asking?' said Rose.

The Nobles looked at each other and with a nod from Diana, George spoke.

'Eight years ago Stanley had a fling and got a girl pregnant. He was married to Elizabeth by then, but instead of doing the right thing, he refused to support the girl financially. He was despicable, so we cut him out of our wills and cut his allowance off. He hasn't spoken to us since.'

'That sounds like him,' replied Rose tartly.

'Here we go,' said Ethel bringing the tea tray through. Ethel poured everyone a cup of tea.

'Excuse me; I can hear Tommy crying,' said Rose, getting up to see to him.

Rose brought her son down and sat him on her lap.

'Oh, what a lovely boy,' said Diana. 'Could I hold him?'

Rose handed him over. Diana sat him on her lap and cuddled him.

Tommy grabbed at her earring. 'Here, give him this,' said Rose, handing Diana one of Tommy's toys.

'We are sorry for just turning up like this,' said Diana. 'Elizabeth said how kind you were to her at the Court. The poor girl is devastated by all of this; it's the final straw and she has decided to divorce Stanley.'

'Well, we have taken enough of your time,' said Diana Noble.

Going into his jacket pocket George handed Rose a card. 'Rose, if you need anything, I mean anything, just phone this number.'

Rose took the card and said, 'Thank you.' After seeing them out Rose showed her mother the card.

'Well, it's true what they say: money can't buy you happiness,' said Ethel.

'I want to know if there are any more skeletons in his closet,' said Rose angrily. 'I don't think anything he told me was true, do you?'

That night Rose told her father about the visitors and showed him the card.

'Well I never,' said Percy. 'George Noble is one of the

biggest businessman in this area, who would have thought it?'

One afternoon Freddie came home and asked Ethel, 'Mum, what's a bastard?'

'Who on earth said that?' she asked angrily.

'Some boys in school said Tommy was one,' replied Freddie.

'Don't you dare say that to Rose.'

'What does it mean, Mum?'

'It's a nasty word, it means someone hasn't got a dad.'

Freddie was thirteen years old but very naive.

That same week Freddie came home with ripped trousers and a bloody lip.

'Fred, what have you been up to?' asked Ethel. 'You had better get those off so they can be sewn up.'

'I got into a fight. They were saying bad things about our Rose, they got me really mad.'

'Sit down, I'll clean you up a bit,' said Ethel.

'Ouch, that hurt!' he cried.

'Keep still, Freddie,' said Ethel as she tried to clean the cut. 'You did the right thing sticking up for your sister but I don't want you getting into any more fights, do you hear me?'

'Yes, Mum,' Freddie replied.

Freddie went and changed his trousers and gave them to his mum to sew up.

That night sitting down to tea Percy asked, 'How did you get a fat lip, son?'

Before Freddie could answer he saw Ethel give him a warning look.

'I just got into a fight at school, Dad.'

Rose asked, 'Freddie, was it about me?'

Freddie replied, 'No.'

'Freddie, don't lie to me, it was about me, wasn't it?'

Freddie nodded.

'I thought so, it seems everyone knows my business now.' Rose got up.

'What about your dinner?'

'I'm not hungry any more, Mum.'

'Sorry, Mum, I tried not to say anything,' said Freddie.

'Don't worry, son, we know you were sticking up for your sister,' said Percy.

'Shall I go up and talk to her?' asked Ethel.

'No, leave her, she'll come down in her own time,' replied Percy.

Life in the Brown household carried on as normal as possible considering the war. Rose's brother George had come home on leave with his mate Harry for a week in January; they couldn't believe how cold it was back home as they had been in scorching heat for months, fighting.

One evening when the boys had been home for a few days Percy came in and said, 'It looks like there will be snow tomorrow; the skies full of it,' as he took his outdoor clothes off and warmed his hands around a cup of tea that Ethel had just made him.

'Great, I'll be able to throw snowballs,' said Freddie.

Everyone laughed. 'Just as long as you don't get the postman again,' said Percy.

'Why, what did he do?' asked Harry who hadn't heard about the postman incident from a few years back.

'It's Freddie's story, let him tell it,' said Ethel.

'Well, one day we had a lot of snow, so I went out to play snowball fights with the boys in the street and we saw the postman delivering some letters across the road. One of the boys dared me to hit the postman with a snowball. He was a miserable old git, always telling us off, so anyway I threw it and I got him right in the face. He shouted at me and I ran off and he chased me across the pond. He fell through the ice before he caught hold of me, then he caught me by my ear and marched me home to Mum.'

Ethel said, 'I opened the door and there with his hand gripped to Freddie's ear he was, demanding that we punish Freddie for throwing a snowball at him. He had a right go saying Fred was a right bugger and we should give him a hiding for what he had done. He was so angry that I told Fred to say sorry and then I sent him up to his room without his lunch.'

'It didn't help when he fell flat on his arse,' laughed Freddie.

'I had to stop myself from laughing. I know I should have been cross with Freddie but it couldn't have happened to a nicer bloke. Anyway when he'd gone I just couldn't help it. I roared with laughter and since then I can't keep a straight face every time I see him,' said Ethel.

Chapter 15

1945

'It's over!' someone was shouting down the street. Everyone had been glued to their wirelesses the last few months of the war; they knew the war was coming to an end. Hitler and his girlfriend Eva Braun had committed suicide that April.

The atmosphere was catching. People began to smile again; at last people had something to look forward to.

Joyce was demobbed and returned home. George had written home telling them he would be home in a few weeks' time. His regiment had suffered terribly during the war and had lost many fine men. George's nickname had been Lucky, because he'd managed to stay alive. Out of the whole regiment only George and five other men had survived from the original unit.

They had a last grisly job to complete before they could go home: all the dead soldiers from their regiment had to be dug up and sent home to their families.

'Bloody hell, haven't we gone through enough already?' moaned Archie.

'It has got to be done; if it had been me there, I'd have wanted to be sent home,' replied George as they were digging away at one of the graves.

'It's blooming hot,' said Harry as he stopped to wipe the sweat from his face with the sleeve of his shirt. 'I wonder how many more we have got to dig up.'

'Dunno, but we can't go home until they have all been accounted for,' replied George.

It was a nasty job: most of the men, the lads had known. They had dug up one of their mates which had been depressing; he'd been married with a wife and two kids.

Swatting at the flies buzzing around the open graves, Harry said angrily, 'These bloody flies are everywhere, they're a real nuisance.'

'So what you going to do when you get home, then, George?' asked Archie.

'First I'm going to see my family and then head for the nearest pub I can find and get completely wrecked, what about you?' he asked.

'Same here,' replied everyone in the grave digging job.

'I can't wait to taste food that hasn't got bloody sand in it,' said Harry.

'You ain't ever gonna eat a sandwich again then,' one of the soldiers said. Everyone laughed.

'Here you go lads, come and get one of these,' the Sergeant said as he produced some warm beers at the end of the day. Everyone dropped his spade on to the ground and gathered around to get a drink.

'Well done, lads, keep up the good work, you'll soon be going home.'

They sat under a tree and drank their beers.

'You heard from your family lately, George?' asked Harry.

'Yeah, I got a letter this morning, matter of fact. Joyce wrote to me; she's out of the Wrens now, she was demobbed two weeks ago.'

'Lucky so and so,' someone said.

'Apparently Rose had a bit of bother with that bloke she married, you know, the one I hit when I was on leave that time,' said George. 'He'd been sending nasty letters.'

'Oh yeah, I remember, he wanted his stuff back from Rose didn't he?' replied Harry.

'Yeah, that's right. Anyway she had to go to court, because he had married our Rose and he was already married to someone else at the time.'

'Bloody bastard,' said Archie.

'So what happened then?' asked Harry.

'He got sent down for seven years,' replied George.

'Bloody good job,' agreed everyone.

'So what's poor Rose going to do now?' asked Harry.

'She's living back home with Mum and Dad.'

'It's gonna be a bit squashed at home, isn't it?' replied Harry.

'Mum doesn't care, she's just glad to have us back safe and sound.'

'It's a shame about Rose,' said Harry.

'It sounds to me like Harry's got the hots for George's sister,' said someone.

'No, I haven't, we're just good friends,' said Harry, his face turning scarlet.

'Then why have you gone all red, then?' they teased.

'So what else has happened, George?' asked Harry, trying to change the subject.

'Not a lot except our Freddie's learning to be a carpenter; he's always been good with his hands.'

'So, Harry, what you gonna do when we get home,' asked Archie.

'Don't really know. I might try going back to being a builder, they probably need plenty of them from what I hear. What about you, George?'

'Dunno, might try my hand at working in the motor trade.'

'Joyce wrote in her letter, Mum has asked if you would like to stay with us until you get yourself settled,' said George.

'That's nice of her, but you're going to be squashed

enough as it is without me being there as well,' replied Harry.

'Don't talk daft. You'd have to bunk in with me and Freddie, there would be enough room for the three of us; besides you know my mum won't take no for an answer.'

'All right, as long as she doesn't mind,' Harry said.

'Well, that's sorted. I'll go and write and let them know to expect the two of us home,' said George.

A week later Ethel received the letter from George. She was thrilled to hear that they would be home soon.

'Look, I have got a letter from our George; he's coming home soon and so is Harry,' she said showing Rose and Joyce the letter.

'That's wonderful, Mum,' said Rose.

'That's good, he's a nice bloke,' replied Joyce.

'Yes, he is, he'd make someone a nice husband,' Ethel said while staring at Joyce.

'Don't start that again, Mum,' Joyce said annoyed. 'If I get married it will be who I pick not you.' She walked out of the room and found Rose upstairs putting Tommy to bed.

'You won't believe what Mum's just said,' moaned Joyce. 'She's only going to try and fix me up with Harry,' she said as she sank onto Rose's bed.

'You know Mum can't help herself; she doesn't mean any harm, she just wants to see us all settled,' replied Rose. 'Mind you, it did me a fat lot of good, look at me.'

'At least something good came out of it, you've got Tommy,' said Joyce as she smiled at her nephew. 'I just wish Mum would stop interfering in my love life; if I want to be single I will,' she added angrily.

Tommy was getting tired and ratty and wanted to go to sleep. Rose tried to get him to settle down. Joyce said 'I'll leave you to it.'

'Joyce, do you want to go for a walk after this one wakes up?' asked Rose.

'Yes, okay,' she replied as she left the room.

Joyce was glad her mother hadn't said any more about fixing her up; she didn't appreciate people interfering in her life, and hoped her mother had got the message.

The family had been lucky: no one had died while serving in the two world wars. Percy had come pretty close, though; while he had served in the Army during World War One he had been gassed and had come back injured. He had been sent to an Army hospital over Tooting way and had spent months recuperating.

George had been lucky as well. He'd caught chickenpox and had been sent home to recover, and while he had been at home his regiment had suffered heavy casualties.

'Mum, do you want me to move out?' asked Rose, one morning.

Ethel looked at Rose and said, 'Aren't you happy here, love?'

'No, it's not that, it's going to get really crowded when George comes home,' replied Rose.

'Nothing will change, the arrangements will stay the same,' said Ethel.

Rose was relieved; she hadn't anywhere else to go. Tommy was three years old and Rose had thought of getting a job, but she couldn't ask her mother to have him full time; he was too much of a handful.

George and Harry came home; they were glad it was finally all over. They came home to a family celebration. Ethel and Percy were pleased their older son had made it home in one piece.

Chapter 16

'Rose, he's a handsome little boy, you must be proud of him,' Harry said as he had Tommy perched on his knee. Harry had heard from George what had happened to Rose. While they were away in the Army George sometimes read his mail out to Harry as he had no family of his own, so he never received letters. There had been no one to write to him anyway.

Harry had always liked Rose; it was a shame she'd got involved with that bastard Stanley Noble, he thought to himself.

'So, Harry, now you're out of the Army what are you going to do?' asked Rose.

'I thought I'd go back to being a builder; there must be plenty of work now.'

'You'll still live around here though, won't you?' asked Rose.

'Yes, I grew up around here,' he replied. 'What will you do now you're free, do you think you'll get married again?' he asked.

'I don't know, who would be willing to take on someone else's son?' replied Rose.

Harry thought, I would.

Ethel had been listening at the door; she hadn't meant to be rude, but she was pleased: she hadn't seen Rose this happy for a long time.

'Well, I had better put this little man to bed,' said Rose.

When Percy came home from work, Ethel asked him, 'What do you think about Harry?'

'Why?' Percy asked.

'Oh, no reason,' said Ethel cagily.

'What are you up to, woman?' He knew that look, she was plotting something, he could tell. 'Don't you go interfering in Rose's life, let her find her own fella.'

Joyce had moaned about Ethel trying to fix her up with Harry. Percy knew she meant well but his girls didn't see it that way.

'Me interfere, never,' said Ethel with a smile.

Percy sat down and read his newspaper.

That night when George came home from the pub with Harry, Ethel collared him and said, 'Can I have a word with you?'

George waited for Harry to go to bed and then sat down with his mother.

'What is it, Mum, is Harry outstaying his welcome?'

'No nothing like that. Do you know how Harry feels about Rose, has he said anything to you?' asked Ethel.

'He likes her, I know that much; he was disgusted with what Stanley did to her,' George said. 'You're not trying to matchmake, are you, Mum?' he asked.

'No, of course not,' Ethel replied indignantly.

'Good; you know Rose would hate that.'

'All I want you to do is try and get Rose out with you and Harry sometimes. I think she's really lonely and hasn't gone out much since the Court case,' replied Ethel.

'Yes, all right,' said George, 'but don't expect us to take her all the time.'

'That's fine,' replied Ethel.

That Thursday George asked Harry if he wouldn't mind going out with Rose and Joyce for a drink down the Dog and Duck.

It was fine with Harry, so that night while they all sat down to dinner George asked Rose casually, 'If Harry and me go out on Saturday would you and Joyce like to go with us?'

Rose looked uncomfortable and said, 'What about Tommy, he can't go.'

'What about him, I'll look after him, it's about time you started to go out again,' replied Ethel.

'Go on, Rose, you could do with a night out,' said Joyce.

Rose said, 'Yes, okay, anything to shut you all up, but I will never go into the Fox and Hounds ever again.'

Rose couldn't face going into that place again; she and Stanley had gone in there when they had been courting and it held nothing but bad memories for her now.

'I told you we were going to the Dog and Duck,' George reminded her.

Saturday night came and Rose got herself ready.

'Come on, Rose, we haven't got all night,' shouted George who was getting impatient waiting.

'I'll go up and see what's taking her so long,' said Joyce.

'Rose, are you ready?' asked Joyce as she tapped lightly on the door to their bedroom.

'I don't think I can go.'

Joyce went in and sat on her bed. 'Why can't you go?' she asked.

I'm afraid to leave the house,' replied Rose.

'Don't worry, you have got us, you will be all right, I promise, come on.' Joyce dragged Rose downstairs and grabbed her hat, coat and bag on the way out.

They got the bus and got off near the Dog and Duck. They walked the short distance to the pub, but once outside Rose froze with fear. 'I can't go in,' she said, turning to walk away.

'Rose, it's all right, no one knows you around here,' said Joyce.

Taking Rose's arm, Harry said, 'Come on, let's see if I can drink your brother under the table.' They found a table and sat down while Harry and George went to get the drinks. 'Blimey, I've never seen our Rose like this,' said George as they stood up at the bar.

'It's understandable considering what that bastard put her through,' replied Harry.

After a few drinks Rose visibly relaxed and she began to enjoy herself. She hadn't been out with George and Joyce at the same time since before the war. They had all grown up, especially George who used to be the joker of the family though he was more serious now, which was understandable after what he had been through during the war.

The night went far too quickly and they reluctantly got the bus home. Harry was funny and charming and Rose felt totally at ease with him. She had told him things that not even Joyce or George knew.

With George the worst for wear, Harry had a job getting him home. They got in and while Harry put George to bed, Joyce set about making some tea.

Rose had gone to check on Tommy, who was fast asleep with his thumb stuck firmly in his mouth. He was curled up with his favourite blanket. Rose kissed him lightly on the head and slipped out of the room and joined Harry and Joyce downstairs.

'Is he all right, Rose?' asked Harry.

'Yes, he's sound asleep.'

'Do you two want a cuppa?' asked Joyce as the kettle boiled.

'Yes please,' said Rose as she kicked her shoes off.

'Same here, please, Joyce,' said Harry.

'Did you enjoy yourself tonight after you relaxed a bit?' asked Harry.

'That obvious, was I,' laughed Rose.

'I can understand you being nervous, especially after what you have been through.'

Joyce came in with a tray and set it down on the table;

handing the tea out she sat down. 'Well, it wasn't bad tonight, was it, Rose?'

'No, I have to admit I did enjoy myself. I haven't done that in a while.'

After Joyce had drunk her tea she said, 'Well, I'm worn out. I'm going to bed. Goodnight, you two, see you in the morning.'

Joyce could see something magical happening between Harry and Rose and she smiled to herself as she went upstairs to bed. It was obvious to her Harry had a soft spot for Rose.

'I suppose I have been using Tommy as an excuse not to go out,' replied Rose, 'but tonight has taught me you can't hide away for ever.'

'Well, would you like to go out with me sometime, we could go to the pictures or for a walk or something?' Harry asked nervously.

'I don't know, Harry,' Rose said.

'No strings attached,' he hastened to add, 'just as friends.'

Rose thought about it and said, 'Okay that would be nice. Well, I had better go to bed,' she yawned, 'see you in the morning.'

Harry finished his tea and crept upstairs to bed, thinking to himself how lovely Rose was, but he knew he had to go slowly or he'd scare her away.

The following morning Joyce asked, 'So are you and Harry going to go out again?'

'Maybe,' replied Rose. 'It's time you found someone for yourself. I noticed you sneaking off last night, I hope you're not doing a mum on me.'

'No, course I wasn't,' said Joyce. 'Besides I did have someone,' she added.

'Who, when and where?' asked Rose. She was a dark horse, that sister of hers.

'You were going through such a bad time of it, I felt it best not to mention it,' said Joyce.

'So, tell me then.'

'His name was Jack Harding and we met when he came into the mess room for his breakfast one morning and before I knew it we had arranged our first date. He was an officer on HMS *Ark Royal*, and he was mostly at sea.'

'So why did you break up?' asked Rose; she wanted every detail.

'We broke up because he asked me to marry him.'

'Joyce, you idiot, why did you do that?' Rose asked.

'Well he was staying in the Navy after the war and I didn't want to be a part-time wife, always lonely and worried, it wasn't for me. All or nothing, that's me,' she said sadly.

'Do you have any regrets, now?' asked Rose.

'Sometimes I wonder what it would have been like but I can't change what's done.'

Joyce was certainly a dark horse, Rose thought as she got Tommy dressed.

After a few weeks almost everyone in the family had managed to get jobs: George found a job as a car salesman, Harry got a building job through some old contacts he'd looked up and Freddie, who was now fifteen, got a job as an apprentice carpenter. He came home every week and gave Rose money out of his wages. Rose had refused to take it at first but it upset him so much she gave in, in the end. Rose loved her baby brother with all her heart, he was kind and considerate and was turning into a fine young man.

Harry on his days off took Rose out either shopping or with Tommy for walks in the park, weather permitting of course. Harry had forgotten how cold the weather was back at home; he had spent most of the war fighting in deserts in either Egypt or Africa.

One night while he was in the pub having a drink with George, Harry asked, 'George, how would you feel if I took Rose out one night?'

'You are, aren't you?' replied George.

'Well, not exactly, we have remained on friendly terms. I didn't want to scare her away,' Harry replied.

'Well, it's okay by me, but shouldn't you be asking Rose?' George said.

'Yes, I suppose so,' Harry replied.

The next time he saw Rose they had taken Tommy to the duck pond in the park. Rose had given Tommy some stale bread and watched him as he fed them.

'Rose, there is something I want to ask you,' Harry said nervously.

'What is it?' asked Rose as she tried to make sure Tommy didn't fall into the pond.

'Would you consider going out with me as more than a friend?' he asked.

Rose had seen Harry for a while and had grown really fond of him; she had to admit she was falling in love with him.

'Yes, okay,' she said happily.

Harry was overjoyed and took her in his arms and kissed her passionately, while Tommy stood and watched them; he thought it was funny and laughed.

Grabbing hold of Tommy and lifting him into the air, Harry said, 'What's so funny, young man?' as he swung him onto his shoulders for a piggyback.

Rose slowly got her confidence back and started to go out again on her own. One day as she walked home, she passed that big mouth Peggy who lived in their terrace.

Rose had heard that her old man had gone off with some old tart who worked with him, leaving her with four children to bring up on her own. These days Peggy couldn't look Rose in the eye; she looked away every time she saw her.

Rose felt sorry for the children but she had no pity for Peggy; as far as Rose was concerned she'd got what she'd deserved.

Ethel had told Rose about Peggy and had said, 'What goes around, comes around, mark my words.'

Although the war had finished it was still hard to get certain foods. One day George had come home with some bananas he'd got off the black market, something they hadn't seen since well before the war.

Freddie had never seen a banana before and when he was given one he tried to eat it with the skin still on. Everyone thought it was hilarious and kept ribbing him about it.

Chapter 17

1946

One night George came home and said in a serious voice, 'I have something to tell you all. I'm getting married to Grace.'

'That's wonderful, son, when?' asked Ethel

'This July 20th,' said George.

Percy congratulated his oldest son and said, 'Grace is a lovely woman.'

Rose and Joyce were happy for him. He had met Grace at work and they had been together for a year. They all liked her, and felt it was about time George settled down.

Everyone was excited about the up and coming wedding, which was five months away.

George and Grace's wedding was a big affair. Grace's father had his own business and George was going to work for his father-in-law.

Rose sat at the fancy reception thinking about her own wedding which had been a hasty affair. No wonder it had been so small; Stanley had probably thought it would have been easier to get away with it. Rose regretted the day she had ever set eyes on him. It was 1946 and Rose could hardly believe that her son was almost four years old; where had the time gone, she wondered.

'Rose, are you all right? You looked miles away, just now,' asked Harry.

'Yes, I'm fine,' was all she said.

'It's been a good day, hasn't it,' Harry said. He had been George's best man and Tommy had been a page boy.

'Look, Grace is about to throw the bouquet,' said Ethel.

All the girls waited to try and grab the flowers as Grace threw them over her shoulder. Rose had been sitting down watching at the back of everyone when suddenly the flowers ended up in her lap.

'It looks like you'll be next,' said one of the girls.

'Not so likely,' Rose said. 'I'm never marrying again,' she said angrily and threw the flowers down and walked away.

'Cor, what's her problem?' said the girl to her friend.

'Don't you know, she was married to a bigamist,' her friend replied.

'No, I guess I put my foot in it, no wonder she was angry.'

After waving George and Grace off on their honeymoon, they all said their goodbyes and left.

Harry seemed quiet on the way home. Rose asked, 'Are you all right, you have hardly said two words to me all night?'

'I'm fine,' he replied. Harry had been standing next to Rose when she had caught the bouquet and had heard her say that she never wanted to marry again, ever.

Harry had planned to ask her to marry him, but had been waiting for the right moment to ask; now it looked like it would never be the right time to do it.

Harry dropped Rose and Tommy off at home. Rose said, 'Aren't you coming in?' after she realised he made no attempt to get out of the car.

'No, I'm going home,' he replied. 'I'll see you tomorrow.'

'You all right, Rose?' asked Percy.

'Harry seemed a bit quiet tonight,' Rose replied.

'He seemed all right to me,' said Percy as he took off his tie.

'I had better put this little monster to bed.' Rose carried Tommy upstairs and tucked him in.

Downstairs Percy said in a hushed tone to Ethel, 'Harry asked me something tonight.'

'What was that then?' asked Ethel, her curiosity getting the better of her as usual.

'I didn't want to say anything but Harry asked me tonight how I felt about him proposing to Rose.'

'That's wonderful news; he'd make a lovely husband to Rose and a wonderful father to Tommy,' Ethel said excitedly.

'Only one problem: would Rose agree to get married again?' said Percy.

'I think she'd be all right, Harry is completely different from Stanley, thank God,' replied Ethel. 'Yes, I think she would agree.'

Percy had given Harry his blessing.

Harry had been hinting all day to Rose but she hadn't cottoned on or just refused to discuss it with him. It was the final straw when she had caught the bouquet and angrily said she'd never marry again. He felt completely miserable hearing her say that, he so wanted her to marry him.

The following day was Sunday and Harry had been invited round for Sunday lunch. While Rose helped her mother cook the roast dinner Percy and Harry had wandered out into the garden.

'Can I have a quiet word with you, Percy?' asked Harry.

'Yes, course you can, son.'

'Rose said at the wedding that she never wants to get married ever again,' Harry said flatly.

'Did you come out and ask her?' asked Percy.

'No, not exactly, I kept throwing hints all day but she didn't seem to cotton on.'

'Well, all I can suggest is you take her out somewhere really nice and do it properly,' said Percy.

'Lunch is ready, you two!' Ethel shouted from the kitchen doorway.

While they sat at the table eating lunch Harry said, 'Rose, why don't we go for a picnic next Saturday?'

'Yes, that would be lovely, I'm sure Tommy would like that,' Rose replied.

Harry's heart sank; he loved Tommy but he wanted to take just Rose.

'Why don't you two have a day on your own?' asked Ethel. 'Your father and I can have Tommy for the day.'

'Yes, okay, if you don't mind,' said Rose.

The following Saturday Harry picked Rose up and they drove to a lovely spot in the countryside. Getting the hamper basket Rose laid out the blanket and put the food out on the ground; they sat under the shade of a tree and felt completely relaxed after they had eaten.

'This is wonderful,' said Rose as she rested against the tree trunk. 'I could stay here for ever.'

Harry held her in his arms and said, 'Rose, do you love me?'

Rose looked up at him and said, 'Of course I do, silly.'

There is something I want to ask you,' he said.

Rose knew what he was about to say and her heart sank.

Harry carried on, 'Rose, will you marry me?' He produced out of his pocket a small box containing a ring.'

'No, please Harry, don't ask me that,' she sobbed as she got up and rushed away from him.

Harry was hurt by her refusal and walked after her. 'Rose, I'm not Stanley, you know I'd never hurt you,' he said. 'When will you start to trust me? We have been together for over a year now.'

'Please take me home,' she said.

They gathered all the things together and got into the car. All the way home there was silence. As Rose got out of the car Harry said, 'Please think about what I have said, please, Rose.'

Rose said, 'Goodbye,' and went indoors.

'Rose, are you all right?' asked Ethel.

'Yes I'm fine,' she replied as she went upstairs and slammed her bedroom door shut.

'Well, that's not exactly the reaction I was expecting,' said Percy from behind the newspaper he was reading.

'Poor Harry, he loves her so much, why can't she see that?' said Ethel bitterly. 'That little boy's the age where he needs a father figure around him.'

Rose came down a few minutes later and said, 'If Harry knocks I don't want to see him.'

Ethel sighed. 'Why not, what has he done wrong?' she asked.

'I don't want to talk about it,' replied Rose angrily.

For a whole week Harry tried to talk to Rose. Ethel felt awful having to send him away.

'Rose, you can't keep doing this to him, it's not fair,' Ethel said after telling Harry the same thing again.

That night Harry knocked and Ethel and Percy refused to be her messenger any more.

Percy said, 'Rose, go and answer the door.'

Reluctantly she went to answer it. 'Yes, what do you want?' she said rudely.

'I've come to tell you I won't bother you again. I have decided there is nothing left for me around here any more and I have decided to take a job in Scotland, so I have just come to say goodbye, Rose.'

Rose was taken aback but was too proud to beg him to stay even though she wanted him to. 'Fine, if that's what you want, then goodbye, Harry.' She slammed the door and stood crying against it.

Harry looked at the door for a moment and walked sadly away. His plan hadn't worked; she couldn't have loved him after all. He felt miserable. He had hoped to make her see sense but it had backfired and now he had lost her for good.

'What is it, Rose?' asked Ethel.

'Harry's leaving; he said he's going to Scotland,' Rose sobbed 'I don't want him to go.'

'Well, you had better swallow some of that pride and go after him before it's too late,' said Ethel sternly.

'Will you look after Tommy for me?' said Rose as she grabbed her handbag and rushed out of the door, She ran over to the bus stop as fast as she could and got there just as the bus she wanted pulled in. She paid for her ticket and sat down. Her stomach was in knots and she felt sick with nerves. She thought to herself, What if he has had enough and doesn't want me any more?

Rose saw her bus stop and rang the bell to get off. She walked the short distance to Harry's lodging house and stood in the driveway trying to get the courage to go and ring the bell. Come on, you stupid cow, go and do it, she said to herself.

The door opened and Harry's landlady answered.

'Hello, can you tell me if Harry is home?' Rose asked the woman.

'Wait there, I'll go and see,' she said sternly.

A few minutes later Harry appeared.

'Harry, please don't go,' she blurted. 'Please can we go for a walk?' she asked.

He stared at her for a minute or two and said, 'Wait there while I get something.'

He came out a minute later and they walked silently over to the park and sat on a bench.

'Harry,' said Rose. 'Is that offer you gave me still available?'

Harry wanted her to say what it was, so he said, 'What one?'

Rose shyly said, 'The proposal. Harry, will you marry me?'

He looked at her and said, 'Are you sure about this?'

'I have never been more sure of anything in my life,' Rose said honestly. 'That's if you still want to marry me.'

'Rose, of course I still want to marry you,' Harry replied.

'Oh Harry, I'm really sorry for putting you through so much pain. I panicked, I thought you'd change after you married me just like Stanley had.'

'Rose, you know I'd never treat you like that. I truly love you and Tommy. Come on, I want to take you somewhere special.' They walked to the bus stop and got the bus. Laughing Rose said, 'This bus is going past my house!'

They got off at the bus stop and crossed the road. 'Come on, I want to do this properly,' said Harry.

'Percy, Ethel, there is something I want to tell you' said Harry once they were in the front room of 12 Primrose Terrace. 'Rose and I are getting married,' he said as he took the little box out of his pocket and slipped the ring onto Rose's finger.

Rose admired it and showed it to her mother.

'Well, it's about bloody time,' replied Percy, patting Harry on the back.

'Well done, Rose, you have made the right decision, love,' said Ethel, kissing her on the cheek.

'Rose, that is wonderful,' cried Joyce.

Freddie hugged his sister and said, 'You're not going to make me wear those stupid clothes that I had to wear at George's wedding, are you?'

'Of course not, not if you don't want to,' Rose said, laughing.

'Ethel, go and get the glasses, it's time we celebrated,' said Percy.

'Here's to Harry and Rose,' said Percy, after everyone had a drink in their hand.

'Can't I have a drink, Dad?' asked Freddie. 'I'm not a little kid any more,' he added indignantly.

Rose got a glass and half filled it up. 'Here you go, half a glass and that's all you get.'

'Well, how long have I got to plan this wedding?' Ethel asked.

Rose looked at Harry and said with a glint in her eye, 'Oh ages, Mum, we're getting married next week.'

'What?' cried Ethel.

'Gotcha,' laughed Rose.

Chapter 18

'No, seriously, how long have we got,' asked Ethel after she had got over the joke they had played on her; she'd almost passed out from the shock.

Rose and Harry looked at each other and Harry said, 'Will a year be enough, Ethel?'

'Well, that's much better than a week,' she replied.

Cuddling Rose, Harry said, 'This time it's for keeps.'

The wedding was planned for the following July. Rose eventually came around to the idea of getting married in church; this time however almost everyone at Primrose Terrace had been invited to the wedding. Rose had argued that she wanted a quiet wedding but Ethel had talked her around saying, 'You only get married once, so make the most of it.'

Technically Ethel was right; she had never been truly married to Stanley.

On the day of the wedding Tommy was a page boy; he looked cute in his sailor's suit. George was Harry's best man and Freddie was an usher.

The church had been decked out with lovely flowers everywhere and as Rose walked down the aisle she knew in her heart that this was how it should have always been: her and Harry.

At the reception Tommy tugged at his mother's dress. 'Mummy, is Harry my Daddy now?' he asked.

Rose picked him up and said, 'Yes, he is, do you like that?'

'Yes,' said Tommy before he wriggled to get down and go off to play.

As they left for their honeymoon Harry said, 'Thank you for marrying me, Rose.'

Rose snuggled up to him in the car and said, 'No, thank you.'

Rose, Harry and Tommy moved into a house near to Rose's parents' house; it was a nice terrace similar to her parents. Rose felt truly happy for the first time in years. So much had happened to her over the years she had to pinch herself to convince herself she wasn't dreaming.

Stanley had been in prison for three years and Rose had never heard from him ever again; he hadn't ever apologised to her. She had heard from his parents that Elizabeth had divorced him. Rose was glad: she deserved better than him.

One evening Rose had come in with the washing she had hung out on the line earlier, when Harry came in beaming.

'What are you so happy about?' she asked him.

'I have heard some wonderful news.'

'Well, what is it, then?' asked Rose as she folded the washing and put it in piles.

'Grace is expecting,' Harry said.

'I bet George is pleased,' said Rose. 'That is good news. Well, it's about time Tommy had a cousin to play with.'

'What about a brother or sister instead?' asked Harry 'It would be better than a cousin.'

Rose was shocked by his sudden desire to have children; she had never thought much about it.

Rose mulled it over and then said, 'If that's what you want, then yes,' as she carried the washing out of the room.

Harry was delighted; he loved Tommy as if he was his real son but he wanted his own children as well.

Two months later Rose started to get that familiar feeling in the mornings and said one day to Ethel, 'Mum, I think I'm expecting again.'

'Are you sure?' asked Ethel.

'Pretty much,' Rose said 'I just need it confirmed by the doctor, I'll go tomorrow.'

'Have you said anything to Harry?' her mother asked.

'No, not yet, I didn't want to get his hopes up until I was really sure.'

Rose went to the doctor's the following morning and he confirmed her diagnosis.

That night when Harry came in from work she cooked him his dinner and said, 'Here you are, Daddy,' as she laid it on the table.

It took a few moments for it to sink in before Harry realized what she meant.

Forgetting about his dinner he swept Rose into his arms and kissed her. 'I'm really going to be a father?' he asked excitedly.

Rose nodded and said, 'In seven months time.'

'Did you hear that, Tommy, Mummy's going to give you a brother or sister,' said Harry.

Tommy smiled. 'Can I have a brother?' he asked.

The pregnancy was nothing like the time Rose had with Tommy; she was plagued with problems this time, constant morning sickness, and tiredness – she felt really ill.

Everyone was worried about her, especially Ethel; she knew something wasn't right this time for her.

Rose grew weaker and weaker as the days passed by. Ethel begged her to go to the doctor's but Rose refused by saying she 'felt all right'.

One morning Ethel went round to Rose's to see how she was, and she was horrified to discover her bent over in agony.

'Rose, my God, how long have you been like this?' she asked, rushing over to her.

'Since this morning,' she muttered. 'Harry had already gone to work.'

'Come on, I'm getting you to hospital,' said Ethel.

Ethel got Rose ready and called the ambulance. Tommy asked, 'What's wrong with Mummy?'

'Nothing, darling, she needs to go to the hospital for a rest,' said Ethel as she got Tommy ready. 'Be a good boy and go and stay at Auntie Grace's for me.'

Ethel took Tommy to Grace's and explained the situation to her before rushing over to the hospital.

'I hope she's all right,' said Grace worriedly.

'I hope so,' said Ethel as she left.

Rose was admitted to hospital where she had a miscarriage. The baby had been a little girl, she had been told by a nurse as they wrapped the tiny bundle up in a white sheet and took her away.

Rose was heartbroken. She had had to go through with a natural labour only to have nothing at the end of it, and she had nurtured the baby inside her for six months. Rose sobbed in her mother's arms.

'Why me, Mum, what have I done to deserve this?' she wanted to know.

All Ethel could do was hug her, she didn't know either. Rose had had more than her fair share of problems in her life.

Harry was told the news and rushed to the hospital. He was devastated. 'Rose, I came as soon as I heard.' She looked so pale against the white hospital sheets. He hugged Rose, not knowing what else he could do to help her.

'I'm sorry, Harry, it was a little girl,' she sobbed. 'They wouldn't let me see her.'

Eventually Rose fell asleep, exhausted by the labour and the crying.

'What can I do, I feel so useless,' said Harry to Ethel.

Patting Harry's arm Ethel said, 'You're here, that's the main thing. Rose has lost a lot of blood and she needs to get well again. You must not feel as if you're on your own because you're not, we are all here to help.'

Rose stayed in the hospital until she was well enough to go home. Three weeks later Harry picked her up from the hospital and took her home.

Setting the suitcase on the floor in the hallway, he helped her into the front room.

Rose noticed the house looked immaculate, and sitting down in a chair she said 'Someone's been busy.'

Harry had noticed Rose had lost her sparkle; she had given up after losing the baby.

'Mummy!' shouted Tommy as he ran over to her. Rose hugged and kissed him.

'He has really missed you, Rose, he kept asking when are you coming home,' said Joyce, who had brought him back from his grandparents'.

'I'll go and make some tea,' said Harry as he left the room.

'How do you feel, Rose?' asked Joyce.

'Empty,' she said sadly. 'I wasn't that keen to have a baby at first, maybe I'm being punished for thinking like that.'

'Don't talk like that, Rose, it wasn't your fault.' Joyce had never seen her sister so depressed; she was worried that after everything she had gone through, this might be the thing that would push her over the edge. Rose was usually the strong minded one out of them all.

Rose felt numb; she didn't care about anyone or anything. She spent her days just staring into space. She neglected herself and didn't care how she looked. It didn't help seeing Grace who was enormous by now and was ready to give birth.

Grace had avoided Rose at first; she felt guilty because her baby was alive and healthy.

Two weeks after Rose had come home Grace gave birth to a little girl who they named Susan. Harry was in the kitchen discussing with Joyce whether to tell Rose or not; he was worried it would make her worse.

'Well, we can't hide it for ever; she will have to know eventually,' said Joyce. 'I'll go and tell her now.'

'Rose, we had some good news today.' She watched Rose's face carefully.

'Oh, what was it?' asked Rose.

'Grace has had her baby, it is a little girl. They have named her Susan, and they wondered if you would like to go and see her,' Joyce asked.

Rose sat on the settee and stared out of the window before saying, 'I'm happy for them. I suppose we had better get them a present for the baby.'

Joyce felt relieved: Rose had taken the news better than she had thought.

'How about tomorrow, we could go then?' suggested Joyce.

Rose nodded and said, 'Yes, okay.'

The next day Joyce called round for Rose and took her shopping. They bought a matinee jacket and some bootees which they wrapped up.

'Rose, do you want to visit Grace and the baby in hospital today or do you want to wait until Grace comes home with her.'

Rose thought about it and said, 'Let's go to the hospital.'

Joyce and Rose took the bus over to the hospital and went to visit Grace.

Grace was surprised and pleased to see both her sisters-in-law; there she had worried that Rose would have taken the news badly especially considering that she had had a little girl as well herself but seeing Susan seemed to help heal Rose's depression.

'Would you like to hold her, Rose?' asked Grace.

'Yes, all right,' said Rose holding out her hands. Grace gently passed her daughter over to Rose who had sat down in a chair.

That day was a turning point for Rose; seeing the baby

had lifted her depression and everyone was relieved to see the old Rose once again emerging.

Harry never mentioned to Rose about having children again. He had almost lost her once and was resigned to the fact that he wouldn't be a father to anyone but Tommy.

Rose visited Grace and Susan often; she loved making a fuss over the baby. Grace never tired of seeing Rose, it was good having someone to confide in she thought.

Three months after the miscarriage, Rose brought up the subject of trying for a baby again, when Harry came home from work that night.

'No,' said Harry stubbornly, 'I can't let you go through that again.'

'Harry, please, I'm sure this time things will be fine,' she pleaded.

Harry refused to talk about it.

Over tea one morning Rose confided to her mother about the situation.

'Well, I can understand why Harry's acting the way he is, he almost lost you,' she replied. 'He loves you so much, Rose, it broke his heart seeing you go through the miscarriage and then the depression,' said Ethel.

'At the end of the day, it's really down to me,' replied Rose stubbornly.

'Do you want me to talk to him?' asked Ethel; she knew how stubborn her daughter could be sometimes.

'Would you, Mum?' said Rose 'I'm sure he'd listen to you.'

That weekend Rose, Harry and Tommy went to Ethel's for Sunday lunch. They had just eaten and Harry was summoned to the kitchen by Ethel.

'Grab a tea towel, would you, Harry, love,' Ethel said.

Harry did as he was told and started to dry up the dishes.

'Rose seems a lot better, doesn't she,' said Ethel as she scrubbed at a roasting tin in the kitchen sink. 'I think Susan has done her the world of good; it's brought her out of her depression.'

'Yes she has,' replied Harry, wondering where this was leading to.

Ethel carried on, 'Maybe it's time Tommy had a brother or sister again.'

Harry's face became angry. 'No, I can't put her through that again.'

'Well, at the end of the day it really is Rose's decision,' said Ethel.

'It's not just her decision, you know,' replied Harry angrily.

'Well, just think about it,' said Ethel.

After drying up Harry made an excuse and they left Ethel's.

Once home, Harry said to Rose angrily, 'Thank you so much for discussing our business with your mother.'

'I had to do something, you won't listen to me,' she spat back.

'I can't believe you'd want to put yourself through that again, you almost died, Rose.'

Harry stormed off to the bottom of the garden and disappeared into the shed.

After an hour Rose took him down a cup of tea. Knocking lightly on the door she asked, 'Can I come in?'

Harry opened the shed door with a solemn face.

'We need to talk,' said Rose.

'We have discussed it; as far as I'm concerned there is nothing more to talk about,' he said defiantly.

'No we haven't,' said Rose angrily. 'Listen, I went to see Doctor Roberts and he seemed to think there wouldn't be a problem this time.'

'You don't know for sure, though, do you?' replied Harry.

'At least think about it, please Harry,' said Rose as she walked away.

A few days later Harry went for a drink with George down the local.

'You all right, mate?' said George. 'You look fed up.'

'It's that sister of yours, she wants to try for another baby.'

'Oh,' replied George, 'I take it you don't.'

'It's not that I don't, I'm worried something could happen again.'

'What does our Rose say?' asked George as he supped his pint.

'She said she'd spoken to Doc Roberts and he reckoned she'd be fine this time, but I'm not sure,' said Harry anxiously.

'Well, if he said she'd be all right and Rose wants to try, why not do it; you know Rose won't stop until she gets her own way,' replied George.

Harry sat staring into his pint, deep in thought.

That night Harry spoke to Rose. 'Well, if you want to go through with another pregnancy that's fine by me,' he said.

'Oh, thank you, Harry,' replied Rose getting up and kissing him.

Four months later she had some good news for him. 'Guess what, I'm pregnant,' said Rose happily. She had kept it quiet for three months until she was over the first stage of the pregnancy. She knew Harry would have worried constantly; she had told her Mother and Ethel promised to keep it a secret.

Harry was shocked: his nightmares had finally come true. He worried constantly for six months until Rose gave birth to another little girl who they named Mary.

'Well, what do you think of your daughter?' asked Rose. She had just given birth, this time in hospital, on Harry's request.

'She's perfect, just like her Mum.'